BOOKSHOP WITCH

A SEASHELL COVE PARANORMAL MYSTERY

T. THORN COYLE

For my Kickstarter supporters.
May one thousand blessings rain upon your life.

Welcome to Seashell Cove, where the waves are treacherous, and the inhabitants are... strange.

1
———

My name is Sarah Braxton, and I'm a witch.

You might think that's unusual, but trust me, I am not the strangest thing in Seashell Cove.

That name. Seashell Cove. Makes it sound like some sweet, sunny town, with white sandy beaches, and toddlers splashing and shrieking, getting their fat little toes licked by gentle waves.

That's not Seashell Cove at all.

Seashell Cove is a craggy, windswept stretch of ocean high up on the Oregon Coast. Cliffs with sheer drops? We got 'em. Waves that will creep up on unsuspecting tourists and drag them out to sea to their deaths? We've got those, too. Centaurs that dance around fires in the forest just outside town?

Yeah.

Seashell Cove is dangerous, cold, quirky, and one of the most beautiful places I've ever seen.

I love it here. I love the town. I love the people.

And I love my store, The Widening Gyre, New and Used Books and Fancies.

That's where I sat, working, on a January Saturday afternoon, with the skies outside the shop windows rapidly turning from dusk to dark.

It gets dark early in Oregon during the winter. Those of us who can, cozy up indoors as much as possible.

I was perched on a tall chair behind the wooden ell that formed the front counter. I was more pretending to work than I was getting actually much getting done. I took a sip from the mug of tea at my right hand. Meh. Tepid already, and how had that happened?

I should've asked for one of those mug warmer thingies for Yule.

Behind me was a long counter topped by wood cubbies half full with book orders awaiting pickup or shipping, alongside a small display of recent releases. On the counter was a display rack of greeting cards made by local artists. To my right was the glowing, outdated computer my tall chair was angled toward. The screen I would rather not be staring at.

Even cleaning was better than this accounting program.

Rain lashed the windows and Main Street was quiet, except for the occasional whoosh of a car going by. I had some ambient "Celtic Winter" music on low to keep me company. Other than my cat, Rhiannon, I was alone. No one in their right mind was out shopping in this storm, and my assistant, Duncan, was taking some much needed time off after the pre-holiday crush.

White twinkle lights surrounded the front windows

of the shop, the way they did all winter, shining on the shop name painted in an arc on the glass: The Widening Gyre. From outside, it would look as if the white letters outlined in black and gold floated above the books on display—a mix of antiquarian and the latest issues from independent and traditional publishers, with a section highlighting Oregon writers.

The lights also cast a warm and cheerful glow on the slender black cat currently also on display in a very undignified position.

"Rhiannon..." I started, then stopped myself. There was just no controlling cats—especially one as strong-willed as Rhiannon—and it wasn't as if there were throngs of window shoppers out to see her bathing routine anyway. The postage-stamp-sized parking lot next to the bookshop was empty other than my tiny, bright orange electric Fiat—that I have to fold my not-so-tiny frame into, but it's worth it— and Delta Crabbit's Prius. Seriously, no one was walking in this weather, not even the most die-hard Oregonians.

The only person in the shop was Delta, acting weirder than usual. Always crochety, Ms. Crabbit was one of those people who had been out in the elements for so long, you couldn't quite tell how old they were anymore. She was a white woman of indeterminate age, but I would place her in her mid-sixties if I had to hazard a guess.

I could hear her skulking around the stacks. Almost furtive. I was just about to go check on her when she scurried past, fake-fur-trimmed hood already up on her olive green rain parka.

She raced through the door without saying good-bye, bells clattering in her wake.

If I were the suspicious type, I would think she was hiding something. But I try not to be, and besides, it's hard to say what's actually strange behavior in Seashell Cove.

With Ms. Crabbit gone, I could really feel the emptiness of the store. Even Biff the ghost was lying low.

All the shops on Main Street were in the post-holiday winter doldrums. Pretty much only the tamale place next door was doing brisk business. People always wanted a break from cooking after the holidays, and besides, the handmade tortillas and chips were the best on the coast. David and his mother, Mrs. Vargas, did good business all year 'round.

My stomach grumbled, telling me what I was having for dinner after closing. Maybe I'd shut down early today. There'd only been one customer all afternoon, the persnickety Delta Crabbit. She'd spent way too long back in the used Occult and Supernatural section, before breezing past me as if I had insulted her somehow.

Something in her behavior really bothered me. Ms. Crabbit was always eccentric, but she wasn't usually that rude.

I sighed, staring back at the accounting program on the computer that was going to need to be replaced sometime this year. And where would I get the money for that? It wasn't that The Widening Gyre was in trouble. Not exactly. The store had done well enough over the holidays to keep the lights on and pay for Rhiannon's kibble. But according to the numbers on the screen, not well enough for much-needed raises for Duncan and myself, and for things like fancy electronics.

A head bumped my shin and I looked down from my perch to see Rhiannon's fuzzy black face staring back up at me. The cat blinked her green eyes and then crouched, giving her butt that little wiggle that expressed her intention to leap.

I quickly scooched the chair out from beneath the high counter just enough to give her proper clearance. The cat landed with a heavy thunk on my jeans—dark-washed and wrapped around my heavy hips and thighs. I'm what a certain type of person would call curvy, and what less polite people would call fat. My biggest fans call me Amazonian, because I'm not only big, I'm tall. I keep thinking that one day I'll take up archery, like my current dating interest keeps trying to convince me to.

What can I say? Stefon is also big.

Tall, dark, bearded, and handsome, he's a member of the Society of Medieval Anachronism, which apparently gives him a thing for women with any sort of weapons.

Works for me. I love a dangerous woman myself. My first girlfriend, Cecilia, is a bit of a dangerous type. Though we broke up long ago, she's still one of my best friends.

As for those naysayers who think anyone over a women's size eight is "overweight"? They can take a leap. I like my body, and always have.

Well, that last part's a bit of a lie. My adolescence

was as periodically angst-filled as any other normal teen's. Thankfully, I was too busy learning how to be a proper witch after puberty hit to let the creeping self-loathing take over too much of my life.

Spell casting and making out with my girlfriend were much more interesting than all the get-thin-quick hogwash, anyway. The dieters tried to shame me for a while, until they figured out I just didn't care enough to bother, and that I had more boys and girls interested in me than their insecure asses ever would.

"Magic conveys confidence," Uncle Cyrus always taught me, and as a newly magical teen, I did my best to take that lesson to heart.

Besides, not only did I have a hot, dangerous girlfriend in high school, I had a posse of friends who had never fit in and therefore, had all stopped trying sometime before hitting middle school. Gaming geeks, band nerds, theater freaks, queers, and the types who either wrote poetry or blew up science experiments every chance they got.

Or they worked on retro muscle cars, like Cecilia.

But The Widening Gyre wasn't magic. It was just an ordinary business in the middle of a small tourist town during an economic downturn. And computers didn't buy themselves.

"What do you think, Rhiannon? Are you willing to switch to a less expensive cat food?"

Rhiannon simply stared, then blinked again. She kneaded my thighs, gave one turn, and settled into my lap to take a nap.

"Don't mind me," I muttered, then went back to staring at the books.

Books meaning those lines of numbers on the screen. Not the books I preferred. Not the ones stacked on the counter around me, and filling the shelves that needed dusting yet again.

That's right, my name is Sarah Braxton, and I run the best haunted bookshop in Seashell Cove.

The fact that it's the only bookshop in Seashell Cove doesn't matter. It's still the best.

I've run The Widening Gyre since Dad died three years ago. I moved back from Portland about a year before that, when he became too ill to take care of the shop. See, it's a place I've been helping out at since I was a kid. I pretty much grew up here. It was just dad and myself, on our own, next to the rocky Oregon coastline. Oh, sure there's my eccentric Uncle Cyrus, and various other family members. But immediate family? It was just the two of us.

And now there's just me. And Rhiannon. I named her after my dad's favorite Stevie Nicks song, and, who am I kidding? My favorite Stevie Nicks song, too. What witch doesn't love Stevie?

Seashell Cove is nice—despite being seriously weird—and Cecilia moved back a couple of years ago to help out at the classic car garage where she apprenticed in high school, but sometimes I miss the excitement of living in a city.

Portland isn't a big city by any stretch of the imagination, but it was big enough to suit me. Cecilia and I both went up there for school, and I stayed. I loved the live music scene, and the art and activism. People were just so engaged there. Seashell Cove? Well, other than tourist season, it's pretty quiet. And that has its charm, I suppose, though it's not always the easiest thing being twenty-eight years old and living in a place filled with retirees.

"But here we are, eh, Rhiannon? You don't care where you live, do you?"

As a matter of fact, Rhiannon loved the bookshop a lot more than she ever loved hanging out in my Portland house with my four roommates. Here, she could curl up and hide if she wanted to, or sit in the window and get cooed over, and get her head scratched by as many different people as walked through the door each day. And when I took her home, to Dad's house? Well, there was a fireplace, wasn't there?

"It's a cat's life," I said.

But was it *my* life?

"You make your own magic." That voice wasn't a memory. It was here, live, in the store.

It was my Uncle Cyrus.

I almost peed my pants.

2

I jumped in my chair, and Rhiannon scrambled up to the counter and then glared at me, annoyed.

"What?" I glared back at her green eyes. "It's not my fault."

Then I turned to greet the dapper interloper standing in the aisle between two bookcases that led deep into the store. The one who had spoken, rudely reminding me there was more to life in Seashell Cove than keeping my accounts straight.

"Uncle Cyrus, you really need to give me more warning before you pop in like that."

He chuckled, the bookstore lights gleaming off the dark skin of his shaved head.

"What's the fun of that?" he asked. "And what's the use of being a warlock if I can't pop in on my niece whenever I please?"

"Uncle..."

The thing about my Uncle Cyrus is...well, first of

all, he's really powerful, especially compared to me. And second of all, we look nothing alike.

I stared at the handsome man in perfect dark blue jeans, crisp white shirt collar peeking out from what I knew was a merino wool sweater in a burgundy that warmed his dark skin, all of it topped by an elegant black trench coat much too nice for the likes of Seashell Cove.

The third thing about my Uncle Cyrus is that he's a lovable, dapper, pain in the ass. A pain in the ass with a heart of gold, a sharp wit, and a bank account I could only dream of.

Cyrus had been my mother's mentor way back when and had apparently fallen in love with my pale, squalling, witchy self right after I was born. He'd been my honorary uncle ever since, though he was only around sporadically, dropping off lavish gifts and buying me ice cream before spiriting off again. Being a warlock was a demanding business.

My skin is fish-belly Irish pale, my eyes are green, and my hair is dark brown—all characteristics I inherited from my mother. I'm big, broad, and tall, which I inherited from my father. And, while I'm no slouch in the clothing department, I'm certainly not dapper. My jeans don't look brand new, and the sweater I have on over my T-shirt is some sort of wool blend, not fancy Merino.

So no, Cyrus and I look nothing alike, have vastly different clothing budgets, and have no immediate ancestors in common. But that doesn't mean he isn't family.

The multiple silver rings on his fingers winked in

the shop lights as he reached to scratch Rhiannon's head. She let him, the slut.

Not that there's anything wrong with sluts. I've been one off and on since college, though there's a little less opportunity for serious catting around in Seashell Cove.

"What brings you to town this dark, rainy afternoon? Weren't you just in Paris or something?"

"I was," he said, in a rich purr that matched the rumble coming from Rhiannon's furry little chest. "It was lovely. And now I'm here, visiting you."

He patted Rhiannon's head and looked up at me.

"Now that I've greeted the shop owner, can I get a hug from my niece?"

I stepped around the counter and let myself be folded into his arms. He always smelled of Bay Rum and frankincense and I loved it.

"I've missed you. And what do you mean, I make my own magic? Were you listening to my thoughts again? And don't you know it's rude to speak to people when you haven't even said hello, let alone walked through the front door?"

He released me with a soft laugh.

"I don't need to read your thoughts, I just need to read the expression on your face, Sarah. Plus, your aura had that spiky-around-the-edges look it only gets when you're worried. And, when a person is looking at accounting software? Sometimes they're wondering how to get out of whatever mess they're in. Hence my reminder, upon entering your fine establishment, that we all make our own magic."

This was an argument we'd had many times over

the years, particularly since I'd gotten my conscious-ness expanded in college, though the discussion had started in high school, when a couple of friends got temporarily enamored of The Secret and I decided it was a crock.

"We all make our own magic except when the larger forces of injustice and oppression come crashing down on our heads, Uncle Cyrus. Or when a bus decides it has our name on it. Or climate disaster. Or war..."

Or cancer, I didn't say, though the words hovered in the air between us.

"Yes, yes, yes." He waved his long-fingered hands, rings flashing. "You think as a Black man in the United States, I'm not aware of all of that?"

I inhaled, readying my rant, but he held up a hand to forestall my familiar objections. "Uh uh uh uh uh. No matter how rich I am—and I'm not *that* rich—I'm still Black. But my point stands, Sarah. Do any of those really apply to you? Yes, you're a woman, but you're a healthy white woman and a property owner. And a witch. So I'm going to ask you, what is the problem with your magic and why aren't you using it to your advantage?"

I exhaled, all of a sudden wishing there were customers to take care of instead of facing this conversation.

"Why are you really here?" I asked.

"Because you needed me," he simply said. "And I wanted to see you."

I looked up at the big round clock over the counter. Close enough to quitting time.

"Want to buy me dinner at the Vargas's, rich guy?"

His smile burst through, shining bright as a late September sun flashing on the waves.

"I would like nothing more."

Soon enough, we were settled in at a table in the cozily lit restaurant with colorful serape tablecloths set under glass at each table. Ours was woven with stripes of turquoise, pink, and black.

The scent of warm tortilla chips filled the air, making my mouth water.

As the parking lot had predicted, the place was busy, humming with conversation over which rose the accordion and deep bass of the Norteño music favored by Mrs. Vargas, who owned the place. Davíd, her son, was my favorite waiter. He set down a basket of the chips, along with two types of salsa, one chunky with tomato and onions, the other the green of tomatillos.

"Thank you, Davíd," I said.

"Need anything else?" he asked as he plunked down two glasses of water.

We both shook our heads.

I loaded up a chip with tomatillo sauce and shoved half of it in my mouth. The vinegar and spicy pepper were tempered by the perfectly crisp tortilla. I was so hungry.

Once I swallowed and then loaded up a second chip, I finally paid attention to Uncle Cyrus, who'd been staring at me the whole time. I didn't care. Nothing interrupts the first bite of perfection.

"Why aren't you using your magic?" he asked, one long finger tracing the condensation on his water glass.

I choked, and grabbed my own water, taking a greedy sip. Then I grabbed a paper napkin from the metal holder on the table, practically knocking over the Tapatio sauce to get there. Patting my mouth, thoughts racing, I stalled for time.

Uncle Cyrus sat still as a snake and stared. Damn him.

"How do you know I'm not using my magic?"

He huffed, as if my question wasn't even worth answering.

I was saved by David, who chose that moment to plunk down two plates of tamales smothered in red sauce. Oh my Gods and Goddesses, they smelled good. My stomach growled.

David hurried off before I could thank him. I grabbed my utensils and got ready to dig in, when I realized my uncle still had not moved.

"Gah. Do we have to talk about this? Can't we just have a nice visit?"

He glanced out the window at the continuous stream of rain and darkness.

"I didn't leave the City of Lights for the simple joys of Seashell Cove, Sarah Endora Braxton. You have been drifting long enough. It's time to take responsibility for your life. You're coming up on your Saturn Return and it's high time you chose what sort of witch you want to be."

My stomach sank, and I pushed the plate of tamales away. Damn him for ruining my dinner.

"What if I don't want to? What if I want to just be ordinary, and run the shop and date Stefon?"

"You do that, and your magic will come bite you, sooner rather than later. Magic won't be denied, Sarah.

You're a witch. You need to help yourself. You need to act like one."

I stared down at the beautiful plate of tamales, red rice, and rich black beans. But I barely saw it.

All I could think of was my mother, dying.

My father. Dying.

"What if it kills me?" I whispered.

Cyrus reached a hand across the table and grasped mine. His skin was cool. Smooth. I loved him as much as anyone, but in that moment? His touch was not comforting.

"It won't kill you, Sarah. Magic didn't kill your father, cancer did."

"And mom?"

He grimaced, but remained quiet.

For you see, magic had killed my mother, I knew it deep inside, though nothing had ever been proven. All that really mattered was that my parents—both witches—were now gone.

And that was enough reason for me to keep things on the down low.

If you don't stick up your head, you can't be knocked down.

3
———

After dinner, Uncle Cyrus had left for the one fancy inn in town, and I had gone home to read a book and watch an episode of *Supernatural* with Rhiannon curled on my lap, and a small fire in the hearth. My cat was no Stefon, but he was out of town all weekend, and Rhiannon had decided to come home with me. She does that more often in winter. The shop doesn't have a fireplace, after all.

But we were both back on duty for another slow, lazy Sunday at The Widening Gyre, rearranging a display of journals in the front window. After the holiday rush, I was kind of happy about that. I'd planned for the lull, of course, and given my one employee a few extra days off, though Duncan would be back for inventory, a chore no shop owner enjoyed.

Money worries still ticked at the back of my mind, joining the image of Uncle Cyrus's concerned face.

I banished those thoughts and ran my fingers over buttery-gold leather stamped with a dragon. The embossed cover was designed to slip onto a fresh blank journal once the pages of the old one filled. The hope was that some romantic would purchase it to write poetry, or deep thoughts, or dreams of a better new year.

Heck, maybe I needed it.

And that was one issue with working in a bookshop. Sure, I got things at wholesale prices, but that didn't mean they didn't still cost money I didn't really have. If Dad hadn't paid off the cottage, I would be in big trouble.

Maybe paying rent on a physical bookstore in the early twenty-first century was a mistake. But it wasn't a mistake I was willing to give up on. Not yet.

And that was the problem, wasn't it? I wasn't giving up, but I hadn't fully committed yet, either.

I slid the leather dragon journal onto the stand, set at an angle that would hopefully catch someone's eye. If anyone ever walked by.

At the other end of the window, Rhiannon dozed again, curled up in a black, furry crescent beneath the lights as I set up the new display. The journals all had varied covers featuring art, cloth patterns, or high-end leather. Mixed among them were a scattering of pens. I made sure to have inexpensive but fast writing ones mixed with colored, thin-tipped markers and a few fancy fountain pens. The lights glinted off the metal, inviting a person to pick one up. Feel the heft and grip of them.

It's the tactile stuff that gets to people. That's why they shop in brick and mortar stores. The literal weight of a book matters. So does the particular scent of paper glued or sewn into packets of the type of magic only writers could wield.

Journals and pens were my latest attempt to bring money into the store. Whether it would work or not remained to be seen, but really, who could resist the call of heavy cream pages rustling beneath beautiful covers, or the particular feel of a good pen?

But yeah. Finances. Not my strong suit.

Having decided Cyrus might be right, I now needed to decide what to do about it. Before invoking my magical abilities, I had to know where to direct them. That meant I also needed to learn some more practical things.

Like how to run a business.

Oh, I'd learned what I could from Dad, but frankly, the bookstore had been slipping even before he got so sick.

I heard the vague rumble of an old V8 engine in the parking lot moments before the bells above the front door jingled and a flurry of hot pink hair and stompy black boots and rainbow-colored rain slicker stormed in.

Cecilia Chen. My ex-girlfriend and current best friend.

"Cecilia! What are you doing here?"

And then I looked at her face. It was pinched with worry, and there were purple shadows beneath her dark tawny eyes.

"Toby is gone!" she said, mopping the moisture from her face with a bright red handkerchief before shoving it back into her coat pocket.

Oh no, I thought, *something bad has happened.* My

heart seized up for a moment before rational thought took over once again.

"What do you mean, gone? Like, they've left you?"

She shook her head, and started to explain, still dripping all over the entry rug.

"Wait. Come on back," I said. "Take your coat off. I'll make some tea."

Clearly, we were going to need it. Toby was Cecilia's sweetheart, a hob of indeterminate gender whom Cecilia loved with all of her motor-oil-stained heart.

"Thanks," Cecilia said. After shaking off her slicker over the doormat and wiping her boots one more time, she headed back, threading her way through the old wood bookcases to our favorite place to visit when it was slow. My dad had set up two comfortable stuffed chairs around a little table beneath a high, stained glass window of a stack of books with different colored glass spines.

This was only one of many groupings throughout the store, encouraging people to read a few paragraphs, hoping to entice them to buy. Part of what we're selling at the bookshop isn't just literature or history, it isn't just spaceships or romance; part of what we're selling is a feeling that you can curl up and be cozy somewhere and leave your life for a little while. At least, that's what Dad always said, hence the chairs.

I had reupholstered the battered things a year ago, with burgundy and gold stripes. Passing the chairs, I went and opened the little office–kitchen combo next to the washroom. A desk flanked by ancient wood file cabinets graced one end of the narrow room. To my right was a long counter held up by cheap, pepper-red cupboards, with a tiny pocket sink, just big enough to wash your hands, or, more importantly, fill a kettle to make tea. The electric kettle held pride of place, tucked next to an outlet. I filled the metal kettle, then clicked it on and opened one of the canisters that lined the counter, sniffing with pleasure.

Cecilia and I had tried to keep our romance going up in Portland after high school, but I went to State and she went to art school, and though our circles overlapped, we forged new relationships. Found new friends.

And pretty soon, those broadening horizons included wanting to date other people.

At age twenty-eight, I'm secure enough in myself that if Stefon wants to branch out, lover-wise, I'm okay with it. And he's said the same to me.

But at eighteen going on nineteen?

I just couldn't do it. I wasn't ready.

It was just as well. Cecilia and I settled into a solid friendship over the years, and now that we were both back in our hometown, I was glad for that. Sometimes friends were better bets than lovers, in the long run.

The water boiled and the kettle clicked itself off. I poured water into the fat Brown Betty teapot to warm the ceramic and put a couple of hand-thrown ceramic mugs, a jug of creamer, and a pot of sugar on a wood tray. Dumping the water, I threw in some loose Irish Breakfast tea and refilled the pot before carrying the whole thing back out into the store.

Cecilia played with a lock of her stick-straight, fuchsia-colored hair, staring at nothing.

"Would you...?" I gestured with my head and she

quickly moved a few books off the small table to make room for the tea things.

I didn't blame her for being distracted. If Stefon went missing from my bed, I would be, too. And Cecilia had been with Toby a lot longer than Stefon and I had been dating.

Like I said, Toby was a hob. A brownie. They were one of those magical creatures that were best at the small, homely magics. Not the big, flashy magic that warlocks like Uncle Cyrus did.

Hobs and the others like them were best at keeping your house or shop running smoothly. Or making sure things were tidy. Or helping your garden grow even under the worst, most neglected conditions.

Some of them went into interior decoration, others ran house cleaning services. The less entrepreneurial minded worked more ordinary jobs, but kept the hearth fires warm in their off hours. Hobs and brownies were good family. It was kind of sweet that Cecilia—with all her bluster and brazenness—had ended up with a quiet little hob like Toby. But the two seemed to balance each other out.

Cecilia had gone back to staring, repeatedly rubbing the palms of her hands on her tight black jeans, short nails rasping at the cloth.

I splashed a dollop of cream into both cups, adding a bit of sugar to one before pouring out the fragrant, golden-brown brew. I handed the sugared mug to Cecilia, who stopped rubbing anxiously at her thighs long enough to accept the mug and nod her thanks.

"Tell me what happened," I said, blowing on the

surface of my own mug. She clutched hers as if it were a lifeline.

"I'm not sure. You know, I'm not a witch like you…"

"But you have magic."

"Not really," she replied. "You know it's too far back to matter."

I shrugged. "Magic isn't always about birth, and you know it. Besides, it being your great-great-great-grandmother who was magic doesn't seem to have affected your talent any."

Cecilia was preternaturally good with her hands, and with getting metal and electronics to do what she wanted them to. I had no clue what Chinese immortal was in charge of twenty-first century electronics, but clearly they watched over Cecilia.

She waved a hand as if to dismiss my words, then took a swallow of tea. I did the same. Tea always helped.

I returned to the topic. "You still haven't told me what happened. And I can't help you unless you do."

And you can't help her as long as you're avoiding your magic.

I told the Uncle Cyrus voice in my head to shut up.

Cecilia hunched over her tea, avoiding my eyes. Why?

"I was asleep. I can't believe Toby disappeared when I was asleep. I always know when they're around and when they're not. It's part of our…"

"Bond?" I got it then. She wasn't avoiding looking at me because she felt ashamed. But as if she were at fault.

She nodded and swallowed more tea, gazing off

again, as if the answers floated somewhere among the bookshelves.

"We went out for a drink or two last night. After we came home, Toby fed the cats while I locked up..."

"And then what?" If I was going to have to keep prompting her like this, this conversation was going to go on forever.

"And then we, you know, rolled around for a little bit. I went to sleep after. And when I woke up for work this morning, I figured Toby was in the kitchen already. But I didn't hear them. And worse, I couldn't feel them."

She began to shake. I set my mug down, then I gently lifted her mug from her hands before it spilled.

"But they weren't there," I said.

Cecilia looked up at me, eyes stricken. "No. Toby wasn't anywhere. And they didn't go to work, either. I checked. Plus, their scooter is still in the carport."

"Then what did you do?"

"I came here." She looked up at me again, eyes wet. "You have to help me. You have to find Toby."

4

Cecilia left for the garage, though how she was going to get any work done today, I wasn't sure.

I had work to do myself.

She had charged me with investigating but hadn't a clue. I mean, really, a hob disappearing from their girlfriend's bed in the middle of the night? How was I supposed to figure out that mystery?

Cecilia had just told me to "use my witchy powers on it." As if.

She wasn't comfortable enough yet to go to the police. And I got it. First of all, queer and gender nonconforming people didn't always feel comfortable around the cops. You never knew if they were going to take you seriously or not. Second, I wasn't sure it had been long enough to file a missing persons report.

Third? The magical community liked to take care of its own. And Cecilia and Toby both fit that bill.

As I pondered, I stalked the store, eyes scanning the bookshelves for misplaced volumes. Some customers loved to pick up books, carry them around the shop, and then shove them into the first space available. Why they couldn't just bring them to the front desk so I could file them properly, I'd never understand.

"What do you think about Toby, Biff?"

The ghost didn't answer, but then, he usually didn't. He showed up when he felt like it, usually when he wanted something. Sometimes he resisted the changes I was slowly making to update The Widening Gyre and let me know by throwing things around. Rumor had it that Biff had owned the shop sometime back in the 1950s and hadn't wanted to move on once he'd died.

The bells over the front door chimed, signaling customers.

I shelved the copy of Louise Erdrich's *Round House* in the used literary section and headed to the front.

Three people stood dripping on the big mat I leave at the front all winter, along with an umbrella bucket for those foolish enough to use the things. Pacific Northwest winds are no friend to umbrellas.

These three wore proper rain gear with hoods, in the classic, muted PNW colors of forest green, burgundy, and black. Forest Green shoved the hood off of long blond hair that framed a round, pleasant face. Burgundy was also blond, and clearly Forest Green's daughter. Black Coat was another teen, Asian, with dark hair cut into a bob that surrounded a serious, heart-shaped face.

"Welcome to The Widening Gyre! Feel free to wander, and let me know if I can help you find anything."

The woman smiled and wiped her feet on the mat. "Do you have a romance section?"

I smiled back. "I do. New is the aisle against the wall, near the front of the shop. Used is toward the back of the store, same aisle. I also have some new releases here at the counter. Rebekah Witherspoon and Courtney Milan are two authors I particularly recommend."

She headed toward the counter to look as the two teens glanced around the store.

"Do you have any books on ghosts?" asked the blond.

"We have a pretty good selection of paranormal books along the back wall, with a smaller section of new books on Oregon paranormal right there." As I pointed, a thump sounded in the back of the store. The sound of a book hitting the floor. Damn it.

Both teen's eyes grew wide.

"Do you have a ghost?" the dark-haired girl whispered.

"Oh, that was probably the cat," I lied.

Both girls looked from Rhiannon, napping in the display window, back to me.

I gave a nervous laugh and shrugged.

The sound had to be Biff, but Biff hated ghost hunters and always kept especially quiet when they were around, so him disturbing a book while not one, but two were in the store? It must be important.

I headed down the center aisle, both teens shuffling behind me.

The most famous haunted building in Seashell Cove is the Historic Kelpie Inn. That 1920s, three-story place was filled with an amazing collection of antiques, art, and, well, strange objects. Whether the ghosts came with the building or the objects, or were just attracted to some sort of vortex, I couldn't tell you.

All I knew was, if you wanted the "Most Haunted Stay of Your Life," you booked a room at the Kelpie. Those ghosts were a bunch of showoffs.

When I arrived at the back wall of floor-to-ceiling books, my eyes scanned the floor. Sure enough, near the squat brocade Victorian-era chair sitting beneath a reading lamp where the two walls met was a hardback book, spine up and pages splayed in a way that made me wince.

"Do you think the ghost threw it?" the blond teen asked.

"That would be so dope."

The teens practically vibrated with excitement. I ignored them and bent to pick up the tome.

Faeries, Hobs, and Gnomes: Magical Creatures of Garden and Home, and Their Uses, read the gilt letters on the dark brown cover. Strange. It was a book I hadn't seen before. Not that I knew the whole inventory by heart but still...

"Someone must have left it on the chair, and it slid off," I said. "People are always forgetting to reshelve books when they're done looking at them."

The girls looked skeptical, arms crossed.

"The ghost books are just behind you," I said. "Let me know if you need help finding anything in particular."

I could practically feel their big eyes staring at my back as I fled up the aisle toward the front again.

Much as I needed the business right now, all I wanted was to brew another strong cup of tea and figure out whether there was actually useful information in this book Biff wanted me to read. Old books were hit and miss as to their accuracy. And frankly, so was Biff. But he did his best.

I had just set the heavy book on the front counter when the shop bells jangled again and Davíd rushed inside, soaking wet, looking frantic.

"Davíd! What's the matter?" Why would he have run from the restaurant next door?

"My mom says the chaneques are gone! Can you help us?"

The teens thundered back to the front of the shop.

"Chaneques? What are those?"

"Can we help?"

The mother reappeared, a stack of three books in her hands.

"Help with what? What's going on?" she asked.

I had no clue, but if Mrs. Vargas needed help, I was in.

I only wished this didn't all feel a little too familiar. Cecilia's partner missing. And now the chaneques...

And me, with a dad who not only quit teaching to run a bookshop on the Oregon Coast, but had been a magical detective, too.

Part-time.

5

I raced after Davíd, followed by the two teens, before realizing I couldn't just leave The Widening Gyre open and unattended. The mother raced by me, then halted as soon as she crossed the threshold, hit the damp outdoors, and realized she had an armful of books. She raced back in, blond hair flying, and dumped them on the counter.

As soon as she was back out, I flipped the door sign to "closed" and locked up, then joined the strange procession back to Vargas's Tamales. Davíd reminded me of a frantic mother duck followed by her young. We ran past the big, illuminated sign that read *Vargas's Tamales, From Our Home Kitchen to Yours.*

Davíd rounded the side of the two-story, white stucco building, past the small parking lot, and toward the outdoor courtyard and main entrance.

At least the rain had let up for the moment, so we weren't all getting soaked, which was good, as I'd left my jacket in the shop and run out only wearing my favorite burgundy fisherman sweater over my jeans.

There was a small garden on the edge of a patio, a cedar pergola strung with outdoor lights, and bolted-down metal tables that looked forlorn and sad, waiting for summer to come again. Bordering the dining patio was a rugged little seaside garden that had been planted by Mr. Vargas and was Mrs. Vargas's pride and joy.

Mrs. Vargas stood in the center of it, in a red rain jacket and black slacks, her dark, gray-streaked hair escaping from its usually tidy bun. She was literally wringing her hands.

I didn't know that people actually did that.

The teens and the mom thundered to a stop at the edge of the patio as Davíd and I raced down the terra-cotta stone path leading to his mother.

"Mrs. Vargas! What's the matter?"

"Our garden," she said. "It will die. The chaneques have left us."

Chaneques were squat, square-faced beings I would see working in the garden at twilight or dawn. About two feet tall, they wore little knitted caps or old-fash-ioned rain hats in bright colors that stood out among the muted tones of the stones and rock formations bordering the garden paths.

"What? When?" I swiveled my head, but there was nary a bright cap to be seen.

She turned sorrowful eyes my way. "They were here this morning when I came to work, and now they are gone."

"I'm confused..." I'd never heard of such a thing. I looked at Davíd, hoping he had an explanation.

He shrugged inside of his hunter-green, PNW-approved rain jacket.

"I don't know," he said. "This is really Dad's territory, but he's on a job and his cellphone must not be getting reception right now."

Davíd looked out across the small garden, toward the cliff's edge. The surf pounded down below and seagulls squawked and screamed.

He looked back toward me. "But I did hear something strange when I was making sure the tables were stocked for opening at lunch."

"What sort of thing did you hear?"

The teens had grown brave and crept closer down the pathway. I wasn't sure what to do about them, so decided to ignore them for now. If the adult with them had chosen not to supervise? Well, that wasn't really my problem, was it?

"I'm not sure," he said. "There was a high-pitched squeaking, and then a thump, maybe like a truck gate opening? I thought it was just some squirrels fighting over piñons. They bury stuff in Mom's garden sometimes. But then..."

He paused again. The pauses were starting to drive me a little bonkers, but I took a breath of the salty air and forced myself to slow down.

I could feel the teens creeping closer still, skinny bodies practically vibrating with excitement.

"But then?" the blond one asked.

"I heard a car door slam and tires squeal away."

"Do you think someone kidnapped our fairies,

mijo?" Mrs. Vargas asked, mouth turned down in a frown.

"That would be bad," said the dark-haired teen at the same time her blond friend said "Who would do that?"

Who would kidnap friendly garden spirits and a hob? I didn't know, but it was looking as if I would need to find out. My hair whipped in front of my face. I held it back with one hand.

Mrs. Vargas looked at me again, her sad eyes turning determined.

"You will help us with this. Won't you?" Though she had asked a question, it was clearly a declarative statement. "You must find these innocent spirits."

David snorted behind her. She whirled on her son.

"They *are* innocent! Like children! They may cause mischief, but that is just their nature. And they certainly cause no more mischief than you did when you were young."

He clamped his lips shut, chastened, and shoved his hands into his coat pockets.

"You will help us," she said again, crossing her arms over her ample bosom.

"But I don't have any experience with this. And what about my store?"

"Can we help?" the blond teen asked.

"We can do all sorts of things," the other one replied.

I looked over their heads at the mother, who lifted her hands in one of those "what can you do?" gestures.

"If they want to help," she said, "I'm willing to drive

them around. They're still on winter break, and frankly kind of bored."

Great. I'd just acquired teen-sitting duty on top of everything else.

I exhaled, trying to combat a growing sense of frustration and unease. I was in no way qualified to help these people, not Cecilia or Mrs. Vargas.

And yet, it seemed that everyone expected me to.

I turned back to the two teens. "You're on. Let's go back into my store. I'll make us all some tea, and we can talk."

"Thank you, mija." Mrs. Vargas threw her arms around me. I *oofed* at the sudden pressure and then wrapped my arms back around her, too.

It felt nice, being hugged that way.

Hugged by someone who could've been my mother.

6
———

Stefon was back and I'd been looking forward to an uninterrupted evening, hearing about his medieval winter gathering and doing a lot of not talking after that.

Then Uncle Cyrus invited us out for an early dinner.

You might think that was a friendly gesture. But actually, it was just his way of enlisting Stefon's helpful self to gang up on me. I took a deep swallow of my pale Oregon Pinot Grigio—my second—and practiced not rolling my eyes. Uncle Cyrus was being exceedingly charming as usual, and Stefon was falling for it hook, line, and sinker.

At least the restaurant was nice. Costa's is part of the Coast Inn, Seaside Cove's one semi-upscale hotel. Our table looked out over the crashing Pacific and the clouds had cleared just enough to get a final slash of salmon and ochre sunset before full dark settled in.

"What do you want to do with The Widening

Gyre?" Stefon's voice pulled my attention back to the table. The traitor.

"Heck if I know," I replied, stabbing at my panko-crusted halibut, wild-caught, of course. I had to admit it was delicious. Cyrus was picky about his food. I stopped chewing because both of them were staring at me, as if waiting for a more acceptable reply.

"What? Do I have something on my face?"

Stefon squeezed my hand, his eyes looking concerned. They were a rich brown shot through with flecks of whiskey. His eyes were beautiful, just like the rest of his dark face framed by close cropped, tightly curled hair and a neatly trimmed beard. He'd dressed up for dinner, which meant a plain black T-shirt instead of a geeky one, worn beneath an open navy cardigan. The only actual dress clothes he has are medieval.

Yes, my boyfriend is a not only a programmer and gamer geek, he's a Black medieval reenactor who can tell you all about historical trade routes and racial diversity in medieval Europe. What can I say? I like 'em smart.

"No," he said. "I just think what your uncle has been trying to say..."

I cut him off with a wave of my fork, then picked up my wine glass again.

"I know what my uncle's been trying to say." I stared at the offending party, who sat there in his sharply tailored wool blazer and his lavender cashmere sweater and calmly sipped his expensive blood-red Cabernet.

"All I want is for you to be successful," he said,

swirling the wine in its fat-bowled glass. "And happy. You have many skills and talents that you..."

I cut *him* off now, almost sloshing the pale liquid over the side of my glass.

"I know. I know. Skills and talents that I'm not really using. Blah, blah, blah." Hmmm. Maybe the wine had already gone to my head. "Why do you think that is, Uncle Cyrus? You don't think it was because I came home to take care of my dying father and then took over the business that was his dream?"

I gripped the stem of my glass so hard I was sure it would snap.

"Babe," Stefon said, "I didn't know you felt that way about the bookstore."

"Oh, I don't really," I groused, taking another long sip of the crisp wine. "I love books, you know I do. It's just..."

They both waited again. Stefon sipped his Oregon microbrew, eyes hooded with concern while Uncle Cyrus attended to his steak. But just because my uncle wasn't boring holes into my skull with those warlock eyes of his didn't mean he wasn't, you know, staring. He could stare with his back turned. I'd discovered that when I was nine and a half.

I stared at the candlelight glimmering in the pale wine. "I don't know that it's the thing I would've chosen for myself. I know I need to work on it, but now Cecilia and the Vargases need my help, so there's no time."

"You can't let other people's problems interfere with your own destiny," my uncle said, neatly crossing his knife over his fork.

"And how do I know what my destiny is? How do I

know helping out my friends isn't it?" The wine soured in my stomach. I set the glass down.

"All I know," Uncle Cyrus said, his eyes softening with a kindness that almost felt worse than his stern gaze earlier, "is that you haven't been using your magic and that's a waste of a prodigious talent."

"Tell me how you really feel." I snorted. "Prodigious."

Then I looked at my kind-of-boyfriend and bumped his solid thigh with my own.

"How about you, Stefon, what do you think?"

He shrugged and slid a finger over the condensation on his water glass. "I think if you have the chance, you should do what makes you happy. I mean, you're not one of those people that has to work three jobs to make ends meet.... Sure, the bookshop isn't the most successful business in Seashell Cove or the Portland metro area, but you pay your bills, right?"

I nodded, wondering where he was going with this.

"Yeah. So, someone in your position has a wider variety of choices than most other people. Right? That's all I'm saying. Choose how you want to spend your days."

I flushed.

"Easy for you to say," I replied, "Mr. 'I'm such a talented coder everyone wants my services and I make a fuck ton of money but still live in a tiny apartment in a sleepy little town.'"

"Hey," he said, reaching for my hand again. "I didn't mean to upset you."

"Nor did I," Cyrus interjected.

Stefon's hand around mine was warm. Comforting.

"Look, I know I'm being kind of a jerk right now, but the stuff with Toby and the chaneques has me worried, plus, two teenagers have inserted themselves into the situation and I'm not sure how I feel about that, and then…"

I stared out the plate glass window at the darkening sky, catching my reflection.

"And then?" Uncle Cyrus asked.

I took another bite of my dinner, some perfectly cooked and seasoned green beans, and chewed while I thought. What did I want to say? And what did I even want? I wasn't sure about either.

"I'm not one-hundred-percent sure yet," I said. "I just want what I do to mean something, you know?"

Stefon leaned closer. I could smell his beer and that warm, lovely scent that was all him. He gave me a light kiss on the cheek and, lips still close to my face, whispered, "You mean something to me babe. I hope you know that."

From across the table, Uncle Cyrus cleared his throat.

"But about your magic…"

"All I can promise is that I will work on it."

"And?" He raised an eyebrow.

"And I don't know what that looks like yet. But right now, I need to deal with the missing magical beings."

Because I had a feeling things were going to get even worse than they already were.

And that felt bad.

7

———

After dinner, I spent the night with Stefon for that much-needed reunion. He's edging ever closer to real boyfriend status, and I could even see us living together sometime in the future.

Maybe the distant future, but the future all the same. Since I hadn't been able to think much beyond the day-to-day for the past few years, this was kind of a big deal. I wasn't ready to talk about it yet, but like I said, Stefon was good at leaving me plenty of room.

I think he knew I was skittish. He'd said once, a few months before, that I should take all the time I needed to decide whether or not he was worth the risk. I'd laughed it off at the time and he had let it go. But I kept circling back to those words, and the feeling I got in my stomach when he said them.

But I wasn't going to change anything right now. There was too much else on my plate.

We had a quick breakfast together, then I kissed him goodbye and left him to his work and headed home. After showering and changing clothes, I threw a load of laundry in and puttered around doing various chores as Rhiannon gave me the stink eye for interrupting her nap. Finally, I scratched her head and headed off to meet Cecilia and the Vargases for lunch. The restaurant was closed on Mondays, just like my store, but Mrs. Vargas had agreed to make us a simple lunch in exchange for a meeting. As I pulled into the parking lot, I saw that Cecilia's classic muscle car was already there, all gleaming deep blue and chrome, next to two other, more ordinary cars that belonged to the Vargas family.

I hurried across the parking lot and rounded the building to the patio used during summer. As I pushed open the glass door, the smell of roasting chilies made my mouth water. Cecilia waved and then stood. She looked slightly better than last time. Her fuchsia hair was styled into proper waves and peaks, but the shadows beneath her eyes were still there, I saw, as I crossed the restaurant. I gave her a big hug, and couldn't help but drop a kiss on the top of her pink hair.

She smelled of motor oil and cedar.

"Where are Davíd and Mrs. Vargas?"

"In the kitchen. Mrs. Vargas said lunch will be ready soon."

I sat across from my best friend and held her hand across the glass-topped table. She stared down at the orange and blue serape beneath the glass. I hated to see her look this way.

"How are you holding up?"

She cleared her throat. "Not so good. I just...

Usually I can feel Toby, you know? Like...their essence. But it's almost as if they've gone off my radar, and that worries me more than anything."

I didn't want to ask the obvious question, but felt I needed to.

"Do you think...?"

That was all I could push past my lips. How do you say to your best friend, *Do you think your lover is dead?* There's no good way to go about it.

"No," she said. "If they were dead I would know it. I mean, it sounds stupid hearing it out loud, and I know people always say that, but..."

"But you think it's true."

She looked up at me, her dark eyes filled with the kind of pain I hadn't seen in a few years. Not since I looked at my own reflection in the mirror after my father died.

"What do you think?" Her grip tightened around my hands.

"I think you would know," I agreed. And part of me believed that was true, but in my gut I also knew that sometimes our wishes colored our perception. Which was another thing about magic, and my current lack of it. I had convinced myself magic was useless, and had begun to believe it.

The thought startled me. It was something I would have to chew on later.

David came out then, carrying two fully loaded plates of beans, rice, and grilled meat and vegetables. Ernestina Vargas's idea of a "simple lunch."

Mrs. Vargas followed with another two plates. David set our plates in front of us and then hurried back into the kitchen, emerging seconds later with a round, covered tortilla holder. Soon we were all seated and tucking into the enormous lunch. Mrs. Vargas must be a stress cooker, or equally likely she was just one of those people that couldn't *not* feed anyone who crossed her doorstep.

Which came first, running a restaurant or the need to cook?

"Any more information?" I finally asked, after I'd stuffed several delicious, savory bites into my mouth and swallowed them down.

Mrs. Vargas patted her mouth with a white napkin and pursed her lips before shaking her head.

"Nothing," she replied. "Except the garden is unhappy."

"Are you sure the spirits didn't just leave?" Looking down at my plate, I noticed I had eaten at least a quarter of my food before launching into the conversation. I must have had a feeling once we started talking, there wouldn't be much time to eat.

And Mrs. Vargas's food was too good to pass up.

"They wouldn't do that," she said. "My husband designed the gardens especially for them. He planted all their favorite things and built the little rock grotto as a shelter for them. They have a home there. He came to look last night, and saw no reason why they should leave their home."

David grabbed a corn tortilla, steam rising from the round container. "They have their tunnels beneath the garden. The grotto is just the entrance."

"Like, burrows?" Cecilia asked.

"Yeah. I think there's a big den down there. They

must be good engineers, because there hasn't been a collapse or any erosion that I can see. And Dad checks it every season."

I looked out the window towards the garden, seeking out the grotto. Sure enough, there was a dark hollow in the center of the pile of artfully arranged gray and brown stones. I wondered how deep it led, and what sort of den they lived in. I realized I didn't know much about these kind of spirits.

Some kind of witch I was. There were a bunch of faery-type creatures living practically next door to my shop, and I'd never introduced myself. Never bothered to get to know them.

Oh, I did admire the garden, but figured that was just admiration for Mr. Vargas's skill. I swear the man can grow anything, anywhere. That's why his gardening business is one of the busiest on the coast.

Or maybe...

"So, like, do they help the plants grow?"

Mrs. Vargas gave me the sort of look a parent gave when they were about to explain a very simple concept to a child.

"Of course they do, Sarah. What did you think? That is their job."

I took another bite of savory beans and washed it down with water.

"So, you think they wouldn't leave. I get that. But what I'm not sure of is why someone would want to steal them."

"Can't you use your magic or something?" David asked. "I mean, not that you're some kind of finder or something, but I know your dad, and your Uncle Cyrus..."

I paused, a green bell pepper slice halfway to my mouth. "I'm not my uncle. He's way more powerful than I am. Besides, he's a warlock, and has a different set of skills."

"So what are your skills, mija?" Mrs. Vargas looked at me expectantly. "I know that you have talent. You inherited it from your beautiful mother."

My heart twisted. Magic. Everyone acted as if it was no big deal for me to use it. As if it wasn't dangerous. As if using magic didn't have a cost.

"I'm not sure what my skills are anymore. To be honest, since Dad died..." I took another sip of water and look down at my half decimated plate of food. "I just haven't had the heart."

And that was the truth.

8

The clouds had scattered, drifting in ragged gray ribbons across the pale sky. The sun peeked through, casting a strange glow on the slate-green ocean. The air was still cold, but it felt good to be out. Felt good to be pounding barefoot on the cold sand. I was bundled in my warmest jogging clothes, wool cap on my head, and gloves on my hands. Jogging barefoot was probably foolish, but it was still my preference.

Stefon jogged easily beside me, his breath huffing out every fourth step. We breathe the same when we run. As the ball of the foot hit the earth, the huff of a big exhalation. And then, four foot strikes later, the breath huffing out again.

The person who taught us this form told us never to inhale when running. Your lungs naturally fill up as the arms and legs pump. All you have to do is remember to exhale.

That's what Mushtaq taught us, and it was true.

Once I learned how to breathe, and to land on the balls of my feet instead of my heels, running became easier.

It was funny that I loved running so much now. I hated it when I was a kid. Well, a teen. Especially after my breasts came in. Give me a corner with a book and I was happy. That was still true, but I liked jogging now, too. Go figure.

"So," Stefan said between exhalations once we'd set our pace, "what's the story with Mrs. Vargas?"

"The garden fairies that live at the restaurant have disappeared. And she and David—and Mr. Vargas, though I haven't talked with him—are convinced they've been stolen. Faery-napped."

"Damn," he said. "First Toby, and now this?"

"I know."

We jogged right, avoiding an incoming wave. We always ran close to the water, despite the risk of getting wet. The trouble with running higher up on the beach was that the sand was loose and softer there. It was much harder to jog on loose sand than packed, damp sand. Plus, higher up on the beach we had to avoid what I called the fallen giants. The huge, twisty, gnarled tree trunks that washed up on shore, leaving their long dark carcasses in rows, deposited by high tide.

Artists made sculptures from the smaller pieces of driftwood, and the park services came along and dismantled them. It was a regular dance on the Oregon Coast, and part of why I loved it here.

"They want me to help, but I frankly have no idea what to do. And now I have two teenagers who are hot on the case as well."

Stefon laughed. "How did that happen?"

"They were in the shop when David ran in, and they just followed me out, along with the mother of one of them. They're into ghosts and all kinds of supernatural stuff. And the mom says they're both bored because of winter break."

"Are you gonna let them help you?"

We jogged in silence for a bit longer because I needed to get my breathing back under control. Jogging and talking still wasn't easy for me. We ran towards where the cliffs jutted out towards the ocean. I could just see the ribbon of light across the sand that signified the river meeting the sea. It was the weirdest thing, that small outlet reaching its finger into the vast Pacific Ocean.

That's what I felt like right now. My own trickle of water was trying to keep its boundaries, but was inexorably spreading out and being sucked into the undertow of the great salty sea.

Yeah. That was magic. You thought you knew what it was. You thought you'd built a proper container. And then all of a sudden you were drowning.

"How can I let them help me if I don't even know what they're helping me with?"

"Come on, Sarah. People come to you for a reason." His voice was edged with impatience. Which was unusual. Stefon was one of the most patient people I'd ever met.

"Oh, and what's that?"

He slowed his footsteps down, and I slowed to match him, until we were both walking, breath huffing out into the cold briny air.

After we walked for a while, he stopped and turned

to face me. I looked up into that beautiful, dark, bearded face. I wanted to reach out one gloved hand and smooth a curl that was sticking up from the rest of his beard, but I willed myself to stillness. I willed myself to stand there, feet turning to ice, and just look at this man whom—if I admitted it to myself—I was in love with. Even if I hadn't said the words out loud.

"People trust you, Sarah. But they also see your magic, just like I do. It shines all around you and in here." He reached out and gently touched the space just over my heart.

I stopped breathing for a moment.

"I still don't see how that makes me some kind of supernatural detective."

"Okay." He held up one finger. "First, you're a helper."

He held up a second finger. "Second, you see patterns. That's part of your talent."

I shook my head. "First of all, I don't see how you know that. And second of all, what does that have to do with anything?"

"You still think I don't know you." His voice sounded a little sad. "Do you? You see patterns. And if part of your magic is seeing patterns, it means you also see what's out of place."

Patterns. He was probably right, dammit. I gazed out at the waves, at the dancing white foam and the shades of green and bluish gray. I looked north toward the ragged cliff jutting out to sea, and that bright ribbon of a river that looked more as if someone had emptied their pool and let it run down the hill towards the sea than any other river I'd ever encountered.

I thought of Toby, and the trust in Cecilia's wounded eyes. I thought of the nature spirits outside the Vargas's tamale house. I thought of Uncle Cyrus, who wanted to meet with me again today. And those teenage girls. They were so curious, so alive. So interested. And what they were interested in was the unexplained. Ghosts, magic, the paranormal. Witches and wizards and all the fantasy stuff that was just my life.

I turned back to my lover, who stood stretching his big, muscular arms overhead. He twisted from side to side and then swiveled his hips.

"Let's head back," I said. "My feet are ice cubes."

He gave me a look. "I don't know why you insist on running barefoot in January. There are perfectly good unconstructed sneakers you could use, or I'm happy to buy you those weird neoprene foot gloves."

"I hate those. They're so dorky."

"Better than your toes turning blue. Race you."

He took off, heading back down the beach, away from the trickle of river, and toward the stairs on the cliff we'd come down. If he was right, what was I going to do about it?

The question repeated with every foot strike and likely would until I figured out an answer. I ran, cold air pushing against my skin, faster and faster, feet kicking up the damp sand, inhaling the smell of bracken and salt and somewhere, a dead crab or fish.

I followed Stefon, darting left and right, avoiding driftwood and the small, clear sacks of jellyfish. It felt so good to run.

The running didn't stop my thoughts, however. I

really needed to start asking some questions, the way Dad used to. And I needed a list of suspects.

Delta Crabbit had been acting stranger than usual. Was she on the list? But what would she want with a bunch of garden spirits?

Except...didn't her family run a Christmas tree farm an hour or so away? Did she need the hob and fairies for that?

Putting on more speed, I overtook Stefon. Tagging his broad back, I raced by, laughing. He laughed back and chased me until we both slammed up against the railing of the stairs, gasping and panting, grins on our faces.

We stood for a moment to catch our breath before starting the hike up the steep cliff face on the concrete stairs that had been built sometime in the middle of the twentieth century.

"I have a question for you," I said, breath puffing as I began the walk up.

He mounted the stairs behind me. "And I have an answer for you."

"What exactly makes this my responsibility?"

He paused for a moment behind me before resuming his climb.

He was right, I really should be wearing shoes. The stairs were rough against my half-frozen feet, and I was getting pins and needles, which wasn't a good sign. I increased the pace, using the handrail to help drag myself up the steep stairs.

He didn't answer until we reached the top and turned to look out over the beach and the dark shapes of the fallen giants. A few people wandered the sand, but there were no kites flying today. Not like there were all summer.

I loved the kites, but I liked this desolation even more.

"You know, in the Society we talk a lot about honor. Chivalry. And, I know a lotta that is white European nonsense. But a lot of it is true. Honor and chivalry are really about taking care of community. It's about what we do with and for each other. Some of the African nations have the concept of Sankofa. Bringing the past into the present to help build the future."

He put an arm around me and I tucked myself against his solid bulk, letting him warm me for a moment before he tugged on me and turned around. Arm still around me, he started heading back toward the car.

"I think you've turned your back on your past, and it's made you afraid of the future."

I stopped us in the middle of the small, mostly empty parking lot, watching the cars race by on the four-lane highway that bisected Seashell Cove and brought tourists in, and out again.

"Dammit, Stefon."

He shrugged and gave me one of his blinding grins. I swear, he must bleach his teeth in secret every morning. "I just call it like I see it."

"Unlock the car. I need a towel."

"Another reason to get some running shoes," he said.

"I hate it when you're right, you know."

"I know." And then he gave me a soft kiss, as if a kiss would make it all better.

But it didn't, nice as it was. I grabbed a towel and bent to wipe the cold sand from my feet.

"I need a shower," I said. "And then I have a meeting with two teenagers." And maybe a wily customer to question.

Feet mostly dry, I got into the passenger seat. After shutting the door, I began to jam my de-sanded feet into soft wool socks.

"Shower at my place," he said. "And then we can go to the outlet mall to get you some shoes."

He navigated out of the parking lot and waited for a break in traffic.

"You're just trying to get me wet and naked. And what about my meeting with the teens?"

"Babe? I'm always trying to get you wet and naked." He grinned as he gunned across the highway.

We were heading in the direction of his apartment. I smiled.

It wasn't often that Stefon got bossy, but I didn't mind it when he did.

9

Stefon dropped me at my place after far too long an interlude. But at least now I was clean, and warm, and, well, satisfied.

But something told me that feeling wasn't going to last long. Not with my uncle, two teenagers, and the case of the missing fae-type beings looming.

I piloted my little orange car down Main Street, enjoying the bright banners and flags flapping in the the rising wind. Seashell Cove was truly a beautiful place, no matter what season it was.

Then I saw her.

Delta Crabbit walked, swaddled in her olive rain parka, head hunched, arms laden with canvas grocery bags. She was heading straight for the Blueberry Café. That was my friend Angie's place.

Darn it. I really shouldn't stop, but I also really needed to talk with Ms. Crabbit. What with the missing hob and chaneques, her stranger-than-usual behavior was really tugging at my spidey-senses. Talking to her was a long shot, but I had to try.

I swerved into the first parking spot I saw near the café, the one car behind me tooting its horn in annoyance. Luckily my car is small and the streets still relatively empty.

I raced through the front door of the Blueberry Café, and was hit by a wall of scent. Cinnamon and coffee. My stomach rumbled, reminding me that a blueberry muffin would be a mighty fine thing to eat right about now. Moving down the narrow hallway to the front counter, I jostled the shoulder of a woman with long dark hair who stood in front of the community cork board.

"Oh," I said, "excuse me. I'm sorry."

"No worries," she replied. Her eyes were a bright green—like mine—and she looked about the age my mother would be if she hadn't died. Late fifties, I would say, with long, dark, silver-shot hair and a tunic sweater in a beautiful blue beneath a long coat. Some sort of Goddess pendant dangled down her chest. She held a flyer in her hands and had clearly just tacked another onto the cork board.

Goddesses for Every Woman, the flyer read. *Curious about your own divine nature? Join us. Send an email to blah blah blah.*

My eyes glazed over. Not that there was anything wrong with women empowering themselves with talk of Goddesses, but that sort of thing rubbed me the wrong way. I couldn't even explain why.

"Would you like a flyer?" the woman asked.

"Uh. Sure." I took one of the purple-hued fliers. I

had zero interest in the meeting, but figured it was the quickest way past this woman—who had a zealous look in her eye—and into the café. Hopefully to talk with Delta Crabbit.

"Do you know what they say?" The question was out of her pale lips before I could make my way past her toward the counter where I could see Delta Crabbit pawing through a change purse. Delta was one of the few people left to still use cash.

"What's that?" I asked, not really expecting an answer.

"They say that every woman has a little bit of a witch in her. Do you agree?"

I sighed. She had angled her body, half blocking the pathway into the café. Clearly, she wasn't going to let me past without answering.

"I'm not so sure about that," I said, keeping my voice light. *I believe in real witches.* The thought fluttered past, but I squashed it like an unwelcome grain moth. "I believe that everyone has their own path to walk. And I don't really care what they call it. Besides, I'm not sure exactly what your definition of woman is, let alone witch."

A scowl crossed her face at that, but she didn't say anything. Just stared. I stared back. Women like her? They often excluded some of my best friends because of a little thing called gender assignment. I wasn't having any of that, thank you very much.

"Well, have a nice day," I finally said. This time she let me past when I took a step toward her.

Luckily for me, Delta looked as if she was settling into stay. She'd snagged a small blond wood table near the window and sat gripping what looked like a large cup of coffee. A gooey cinnamon roll sat in front of her, a fork poised to dig in, a look of expectation on her rough, weathered face.

"Hey Angie!" I greeted the shop owner, a strapping white woman like myself, though her hair was washed-out blond and tied back with a blue kerchief. She wore a blue apron to match. Everything in the Blueberry Café was festooned with splashes of rich blueberry-blue. The rest of the space behind the counter was white tile and chrome, though the small dining area was filled with the surprisingly comfortable blond wood chairs, benches, and tables, Scandinavian style.

"What'll it be today?" she asked. Angie seemed a bit distracted, which, considering how few customers were around, seemed strange.

"Six blueberry muffins if you've got them, or a variety if you don't." I handed her my credit card. "Is everything okay?"

"What?" She looked up from the register. "Oh. Yeah. Just...someone smashed up our greenhouse last night."

"What? Could it have been animals?" But the sinking sensation in my stomach told me what her answer would be.

She shook her head. "The only animal that could've done that was a human or a bear. And the black bears don't usually come into town. Besides, they should be hibernating right now."

"Who would do that to you?" I asked. It made no sense. Everybody loved the Blueberry Café.

"I only wish I knew." She looked out across the café to the front windows and the shops of Main Street. Her eyes looked worried. "At any rate, I'll get your order ready."

"I'll be right back."

Angie nodded and snapped open a crisp white bakery bag, and picked up a pair of tongs as I turned away.

I wove my way through the mostly empty café tables, accompanied by the friendly noises of the hissing milk frother, teaspoons stirring sugar into coffee, and some classic Run DMC over the loudspeakers. Strange choice, but at least it would keep the baristas awake.

"Ms. Crabbit?" I asked, hovering over her table. She startled and looked up, a flake of white icing stuck to the right corner of her thin lips. The green knit cap tucked over her head was fraying and pilled. Was Ms. Crabbit having money issues? Should I pay better attention to her?

"Sarah," she said, more as if she was reminding herself of my name than greeting me.

She didn't offer me a chair, which was just as well. I didn't have time to sit. But now that I was standing here, with Delta Crabbit looking up at me, I felt foolish. I had no clue what in the world I was even going to ask her. I clutched the darn purple flyer in one hand and tugged at the scarf around my neck, suddenly too warm in the steamy café.

"Do you know much about gardening?" I blurted.

Her pale brown eyes clouded, and she wrinkled her brow in confusion before shaking her head.

"Not much. That would be Mr. Vargas you need. He knows everything about gardening."

She looked at me as if I'd run outside in nothing but my underpants.

I nodded. "I know that, but didn't someone tell me your family owned a Christmas tree farm?"

She shrugged. "Christmas tree farms are different. And besides, there's workers for that. All I do is keep the books."

"Do you have any...you know, elves or something out there?"

She sniffed, and crossed her arms over her sweater. "Elves. Hey, why are you asking, anyway? Christmas is over."

"Just wondering," I said. "I'm always trying to learn new things." Wow. Was I just spewing out random words, or what?

"Sarah! Your muffins are ready." Saved by the bell, or Angie's voice, thank the Gods and Goddesses.

"You have a good day, Ms. Crabbit."

Delta Crabbit just shook her head again and grumbled before turning back to her cinnamon roll.

I didn't blame her. I was the one acting strangely now, even for me, and I was no competition for a warm, Blueberry Café pastry.

Besides, everyone knew that elves had nothing to do with growing plants.

10

———

There wasn't enough tea in all the world.

Not to deal with Uncle Cyrus when he was in one of his moods. And wow, was he in a mood right now.

I stood on an anti-fatigue mat behind the counter, mug cradled in my hands, watching Uncle Cyrus pace back and forth, as if trying to wear a hole in the hardwood floors of The Widening Gyre. If anyone could put a dent in the fifty-plus-year-old boards, he could. His hard-soled shoes *tap tap tapped*, then swished as he turned.

One carrot muffin was already a small pile of crumbs and empty paper wrapper in the bottom of the kitchen trash can. The bag from Angie's still called to me, reminding me of the tasty treats within, the ones I was saving for the teens when they finally arrived.

And where were they, anyway?

I took a a sip of tea—spiced masala chai today— sighed, and set the mug down on the counter and continued pricing books, which is what I'd been doing when Cyrus arrived.

I'd hauled a stack of used books out from the storage room. They'd been waiting around for at least two months. That's how far behind I was and, having finally gotten to the bottom of the books, the finances weren't getting any better. It turns out that caring for a sick parent didn't make for business success.

Which meant I did not have time to deal with the upheaval.

"You can't avoid this forever," Uncle Cyrus said, irritation stamped all over his face. He waved his elegant fingers and sparks flew. Literally. Great. Just great. Not only was Cyrus in a snit, he was unconsciously using his magic. And for a warlock as controlled and experienced as my uncle was, this was a Very. Bad. Sign.

"You're sparking."

"What?"

I pointed at the fingers of his right hand. He shook them off, sending orange and blue sparks everywhere. Two of them landed on the counter and I smacked them before they could set fire to any of the books.

Occult Philosophy was the book in front of me. It was one of those old books from the 1960s, with a semiserious cover. Magic books from that era came in two flavors: lurid and sensational, or serious and trying too hard.

This was one of the *trying too hard* variety, filled with stories from the era of Madame Blavatsky all the way back to Paracelsus, pretending it was all true.

Oh, not that those people didn't exist. They did. And not that magic workers didn't exist during those time periods, because they did, too. But mostly, there were people who *thought* they were magic workers. What they were doing wasn't real magic. Not the kind I'm talking about.

A lot of it was flights of fancy, some of it was garden-variety human psychic skills and the development of innate human talents, but the rest?

It was what my father used to call hogwash. As long as there weren't customers in the store at the time.

"Are you even paying attention?"

"Sure," I said, looking up again.

"So what did I just say?" That thing that people call a thunderous brow? Uncle Cyrus had it, and it was directed at me.

I sighed again and picked up my spiced tea. "I already said I agreed with you. What more do you want from me?"

He came forward and leaned against the counter. I could smell his aftershave. It always struck me as funny that he could afford the most expensive cologne in the world and still used plain old Bay Rum.

Although in the moment Cyrus also smelled a bit like magic, singed around the edges.

"I want to know what your Plan is," he said. There was clearly a capital-P on that word *plan*.

I climbed up on the high stool behind the counter and put my head in my hands.

"I don't know Uncle Cyrus. Why don't you tell me? All I know is my best friend is in crisis because her partner is missing, and the sprites were stolen from the garden next door, and someone busted up Angie's greenhouse...."

"And?"

"And I honestly don't know what to do. I need your help."

He was silent. I chanced a look up, and sure enough, his thunderous brow had been replaced by a smug look. The kind Rhiannon got when she knew she could pull something over on me.

"Dammit," I said, "you tricked me."

He shrugged. "A warlock uses all the tools at his disposal to get what he desires."

I could tell he was quoting again, probably some early magical training manual that I had failed to read, or had read so long ago I'd forgotten it.

"How about witches? What do witches need to do?"

He cupped one of the hands that still clutched my tea mug. His touch was actually gentle. Kind.

"Sarah, it's time I told you what really happened to your mother."

Ice raced up my spine at his words. I clenched my stomach muscles, as if bracing for a blow.

The bells over the front door jangled and a burst of cold air followed by a rush of laughter disturbed the moment. I quickly withdrew my hand and turned.

"And who is this?" Uncle Cyrus asked, straightening. He sniffed, as though scenting the air, which was a little bit weird.

The two teens stood panting in the entryway, faces bright with excitement, two sets of cheeks—one pale gold, the other paler cream—were tinged with rose from the cold.

"Hi," the blond stepped forward. "I'm Tracy."

"And I'm Tabitha," said the other teen, shucking off her black jacket.

Their names were Tracy and Tabitha? What in the world…?

At least Tracy's name wasn't Sabrina.

"We came to help Sarah," Tracy said, shoving her mittens into the pockets of her coat.

"Well," Uncle Cyrus said, "isn't that delightful? You are here to help Sarah with what?"

"She said we could help her find the…I can't remember what they're called." Tracy turned to Tabitha.

"Chaneques."

Uncle Cyrus's eyebrows rose to his nonexistent hairline.

"You didn't tell me that the spirits that were missing were chaneques."

I shrugged and shook my head. "Why? Is that important?"

"A hob and a troop of chaneques? That is a very interesting combination. They are very different types of being."

"I know that," I said, irritated. Because I did know that, but hadn't thought that it was strange at all.

So either someone had a need for a variety of small magics for some reason…

Or they were targeting people close to me.

11

The teens' timing could not have been worse.

What did Uncle Cyrus mean, he needed to tell me something about my mother's death? The thought ping-ponged in my brain, back-and-forth, back-and-forth, as if greased imps wielded the paddles. I stifled a groan.

The doors opened, setting the bells to jingling again, and there was my handsome maybe-boyfriend, hood up, hands stuffed in his jacket pockets. He filled the doorway and looked good enough to eat.

His head whipped around from person to person, and he gave my uncle a nod.

"Stefon, what are you doing here? I thought you had a deadline."

He glanced at Tabitha and Tracy again and hurried over to the counter. He leaned across and motioned for me to come closer.

And it didn't seem like he wanted a kiss.

"There's trouble," he said, keeping his voice low.

"What kind of trouble?" I asked

Cyrus sidled closer, although with his superior hearing he didn't really need to.

"Stefon?" I asked.

"Can we go in the back? he said. "I don't want to…"

"We can hear you," Tabitha said. "And you should know, whoever you are, that we are here to help Sarah. She said we could."

He looked up, startled, his head whipping back around where the two teens stood, arms crossed in front of their chests. They stared back.

"Who are you?" he asked. So smooth.

Tracy cocked a hip. "And who are you? And what relationship do you have with Sarah here?"

I threw up my hands. "Stop. Everybody."

The nerve of teenagers. I looked at Uncle Cyrus.

"Was I ever that bad?"

He gave a rough chuckle. "You have no idea."

I took that to mean I was worse. Ha. I didn't see how that could be true, but what did I know? I mean, much as every magic practitioner tries to follow the dictum "know thyself," it's one of the hardest things to do.

"Sarah?" Stefon said. "What's going on?"

I sighed again—I was doing that a lot, lately— exited from around the counter, walked across the store, and snicked the latch closed on the front door. Then I flipped the sign.

I looked at Tabitha and Tracy and pointed towards the back. "You two. Get enough chairs for everybody and bring them to the alcove under the stained glass, please." The girls nodded and scurried off.

"You." I pointed to Uncle Cyrus. "I want you to

figure out exactly what information we need to know to deal with these situations, whatever they are." Cyrus *humphed*, letting me know exactly how much he liked being ordered around, but headed toward the alcove all the same.

"And you." I looked down to where Rhiannon was suddenly weaving around my legs, depositing black fur on my jeans. "Go to the front of the shop. Keep watch, please."

She blinked her beautiful green eyes at me, licked a paw, and then padded back to the front window where she leapt up and sat, actually alert this time. Amazing. Maybe I *was* a powerful witch.

"What about me?" Stefon said.

"You're going to help me make tea."

I could hear the teens scraping chairs across the beautiful wood floors, and winced. Oh well. That was the price I paid for enlisting them, wasn't it? Or not ordering them home, was more like it.

I assumed Cyrus was ensconced in one of the comfortable chairs in the alcove. He'd better be cooking up a good explanation for all of this. I cursed inside, knowing we wouldn't be able to talk about what I really wanted to for quite some time. I really wanted to know what he meant about my mom.

I led Stefon back to the office/work room/tiny shop kitchen. We crowded in and I dumped the old water out of the kettle, and refilled it as he leaned against the counter.

"Would you get some mugs out? And the teapot?"

He startled but then did as I asked. As we worked, I finally spoke again. "What's the emergency?"

"You know my friend Rolf?"

"From the SMA?" Another one of Stefon's medieval reenactor friends.

"Yeah. Well, he called me, frantic, and said his grandmother had disappeared."

"His grandmother? Did he call the police?"

"He insisted he didn't want to."

That made no kind of sense. The kettle clicked and I poured a splash of boiling water to prime the squat Brown Betty pot. I needed a strong tea. Irish Breakfast. The teenagers could be stunted from caffeine for all I cared.

"Do you know why?"

He shook his head, brow creased. "He asked me to call you. Set up a meeting for tonight."

I set the pot down on the counter.

"Stefon? What the hell is going on?"

"I only wish I knew. What's happening here? You were all acting like something was up."

"Do you have time to stay and find out? You probably should."

In case all of these disappearances were connected.

I put tea into the pot and filled it, and he started loading up the tray with mugs, including one for himself. He was staying, then.

I got out milk and sugar, and plonked them on the tray along with the bag of muffins. I should put the baked goods on a plate, but couldn't be bothered.

"I might as well," he said, picking up the tray as if it wasn't loaded down with crockery at all. I needed to up my workout game. Or just have Stefon always carry the heavy stuff. "I'm too preoccupied to concentrate on coding today. Besides, my deadline just got extended. Customer keeps changing what they want."

I heard that groan he didn't make out loud. Customers were Stefon's bread and butter, and the bane of his existence. He would've been much happier just coding games for himself, but he wasn't quite entrepreneurial enough for the pressure. Yet.

Speaking of...

Before I opened the door, I turned again. "You know how you always say you're risk averse?"

"Yeah," he said. "I prefer strategy and tactics and long-term thinking to short-term, unknown gains."

I opened the door wide and I motioned him through. "I think you're going to be put to a test right now."

"Good thing I'm trained in battle, then."

"Good thing."

I led the way toward the murmur of voices, passing through a cold spot.

Biff the ghost was on the watch.

"We'll all need whatever battle training we can come by. I can feel it in my bones."

And like the ghost, we were all going to need to be alert.

12

———

Stefon piloted his car up from the highway, headlights reflecting on house windows as we headed into the hills. This wasn't the same street his apartment building was on, but I could tell we were climbing just as high.

The heater warmed my toes and the rain fell steadily in the growing dark, washing out the paint colors on the front doors of people's homes. It wasn't worth it to paint houses bright colors in this sort of climate, so people made do with dressing up their doors, protected from the elements by porch roofs, large and small.

There were three places to live in Seashell Cove. One, high up with ocean views. Two, low down with ocean views. Three, everywhere else—aka, places without ocean views.

I lived in an AKA neighborhood. Dad had done well for himself, but not well enough for the view. At least, not from the house. There was a small slice of ocean view from one corner of the tiny backyard, which I loved.

The meeting at the bookshop had been a disaster. Uncle Cyrus had growled, terrifying the teens. I had snapped back at him, terrifying Stefon. We didn't get very far before Tracy's mom, Carol, showed up to fetch them both for dinner, which they seemed hungry for, despite the muffins. Uncle Cyrus had an appointment of some sort as well, which frankly was a relief.

So Stefon and I ate dinner ourselves—soup at his place—and were now heading to his friend Rolf's home see about the case of the missing grandparent. We soon pulled up into what might have been an ordinary house if it weren't for being firmly in a "has a great view" neighborhood. Two stories, built sometime in the last two decades, and only slightly battered by the weather. It took a lot of money to keep things looking that good in Seashell Cove.

I unbuckled my seatbelt but didn't open the door, and I noticed Stefon hadn't either.

I turned to him. "You okay?"

He shook his head, then exhaled and grabbed my hand without looking. He does that. Stefon is a touchy-feely type. Nothing calms or comforts him more than any kind of physical connection. Lucky for me, I like it.

We both stared at the house through the rain-mottled windshield, at the peeling, light gray paint that covered what should have been fake siding but which the people who constructed it had foolishly covered with wood. The house had a nice, broad porch, which would be handy for bringing in groceries on the hundred and eighty days it rained here. The door was painted forest green.

"You know me," he finally said, his fingers playing with mine. "I think I'm fine with the magic stuff, but then…"

"But then things get complicated," I finished.

"Yeah," he said. "Complicated."

"Well, the only way out is through."

He released my hand and opened his car door. "Into the breach."

As we approached the broad porch and the green door, I couldn't help but wonder when my life had taken a left turn like this. And then I realized that the truth was, Dad must've been protecting me, and then the busyness of the fallout of grief and trying to keep the store going had been a reprieve of sorts.

I hadn't had to deal with the magical world at all, I realized. Not since Mom died. So I hadn't even really needed to abandon anything.

I also realized that this was what likely my life was going to be like from now on. Dealing with magic and its fallout, the way both my parents had.

"I hope not," I whispered into the pattering rain. I mounted the steps.

"What was that?" Stefon asked, just as the door opened and there stood his friend, saving me from answering.

Rolf was tall, pale, skinny, and red-haired. His feet were bare and he wore a red-and-blue patterned sweater over faded jeans. His red goatee looked as if a squirrel had been combing it and his greenish-blue eyes were bloodshot.

"Hey," he said, "thanks for coming."

We wiped our boots on the outside mat and once inside, bent to remove them, shuffling next to each other in the entryway. There was a pile of shoes in a boot tray just inside the door. Stefon and I left ours there before padding after Rolf down a long, white hallway hung with family portraits. Doors opened off either side, but we headed toward the light at the end, where the hall opened into one big room. It was spectacular, and showed that Rolf really did come from money, or made a lot of money on his own.

I realized I had no idea what Stefon's friend did for work. We'd met only at a couple of the SMA camping events, and people there didn't turn to talk about what they called "the mundane world."

Campfire conversations focused on the battles that had taken place that day—who had fought well and who had been injured, and who had made a right ass of themselves, entertaining the rest of the populace. Other people were engaged with storytelling, music, soap making, embroidery, or the like, and most could talk your ear off about their specialty. It was kind of a nice respite from the rest of the contemporary world. And one I wouldn't mind getting back to soon.

Once all of this was done.

But I had to admit I far preferred Dad's cozy cottage to this big open space, no matter how inviting the fire in the floor-to-ceiling slate fireplace was, and how lush the contemporary furniture was, and regardless of what was surely an astonishing ocean view during daylight hours.

Rolf motioned us toward a big, L-shaped cream

sectional sofa strewn with burgundy-and-blue patterned throw pillows. There was also one of those massive padded ottoman-type coffee tables in the center of the couch and two chairs.

Rolf puttered about in the kitchen. I glanced at Stefon and raised an eyebrow in question, wondering if we should help. He just shrugged and settled deeper into the sofa. I guess that was my answer.

Soon enough, Rolf was back, carrying a big wooden tray filled with mugs and both a teapot and coffeepot on offer, along with a fat honey bear, a sugar bowl, and two different kinds of creamer.

"There is half-and-half and oat milk," he said, gesturing to the two small white pots. Then he slid onto the sofa and crossed a bare, pale foot over one jean-clad knee. With one arm stretched across the sofa back, he stared absently at the reflections in one of the big dark windows, as if waiting for something.

As if he hadn't been the one to call us here.

Stefon leaned over the ottoman coffee table thingy, lifting first the coffeepot, and then the teapot. I gestured towards the tea. He poured a mug of each beverage, and fixed mine the way he knew I liked it in the evening, with some oat milk and half a teaspoon of raw sugar. Then he doctored his own coffee.

"Rolf? Coffee or tea?"

Rolf started and jerked his head towards Stefon.

"What? Oh coffee. Thanks."

I cleared my throat and picked up my mug of tea. A hand-thrown ceramic mug with a brown and blue glaze, it was the type the merchants sold at the SMA events I had attended.

"So what happened with your grandmother?" I asked. I figured if I didn't get the ball rolling, no one would.

He looked out the window again, long, pale fingers wrapping his cup of coffee.

I throttled down a sigh, but wondered how long this was going to take. I shot Stefon a look. This was his friend, after all.

"Hey," Stefon said, voice soft. He spoke as if he were talking to a wild animal and didn't want to frighten it. "Tell us. We'll help you if we can, you know that."

Rolf took a sip of coffee, grimaced, then nodded. He leaned forward, placing both feet on the sisal carpet, cradling his cup between his hands.

"I went to take her out for brunch as usual, and she wasn't there. At least, she wasn't answering the door. So I let myself in, and it was as if she had just walked out and not come back."

"Do you think she had been there earlier in the morning?" I asked.

"No, it was clear she hadn't been. I even looked to see if the sink or shower were wet but they weren't, and there wasn't her usual teacup in the kitchen sink, either."

"Was anything missing?" Stefon asked.

"That was the weird thing. Even her purse was by the front door, on the console table, the way it usually is. None of her clothing was missing except the red jacket I just got her for Yule. And her keys. Her keys weren't in the dish on the console."

"What do you think happened?"

"Either she had a sudden brainstorm and walked out into the rain, or someone kidnapped her."

Maybe there's another answer, I thought. *Maybe she's been taken into faery instead.*

Rolf hunched his skinny shoulders, and blew across his coffee.

The list of things we didn't know was growing longer, but the glimmerings of witch's intuition stirred inside me.

"I think we should go look."

13

———

"Are you sure about this?"

Stefon looked down at me, forehead creased with concern. I tucked my hair more firmly under my burgundy wool watch hat. We had stayed with Rolf until late, talking, and it was now morning. The store's post holiday winter hours were eleven to five, so there should be plenty of time to do the search and for Stefon and I to get back to our respective day jobs.

"Nope. But I don't see any way around it at this point."

Except to leave this barren cliff top just south of the town's borders. To close the shop, go home to my cozy cottage, make some hot chocolate, and curl up with Stefon on the sofa to binge watch old seasons of *Supernatural.*

Every single episode. For as many days as it took.

Until this problem went away. All the problems, including whatever Uncle Cyrus still needed to tell me about my mom.

Speaking of Cyrus, I'd left him a message, letting him know where we were in case something bad happened and asking him to meet us if possible. Rolf had offered himself as backup, but I politely refused. I wanted Rolf out of the way for a few reasons. First, what if his grandmother wandered home and needed help? Or social services called?

But mostly, what if his grandmother's body was at the bottom of a cliff wall?

Since my intuition wasn't giving me any more information than "go to this place and look for this significant something-or-other," it was best he stay behind.

Dread filled my bones. I really didn't want to see someone's grandma splayed out on a rock, you know? Forget staying home and binge watching television, maybe Stefon and I needed a vacation. We'd never...

"Babe?"

I jerked. I'd been staring off at the cloud-obscured horizon as if I really could leave. Dodge the question of my magic. Leave the missing hob and chaneques to their own devices. Forget about Angie's smashed-up greenhouse and Rolf's grandmother.

Disappoint my family and friends.

"Sorry," I said, then gave him a quick kiss. "I'm ready."

I took a step toward the tiny cut between two rocks that couldn't really be called a path, but it seemed to be where my gut was pulling me. A scrubby piece of grass waved forlornly.

I gave a small wave in reply. A tiny scrap of what looked like brown denim was caught in a bush just down below. And were those tiny footprints? Or was I making up details that just weren't there, hoping my gut was right?

"Why aren't you using the steps? Over there?" Stefon's voice was patient. Reasonable.

I stopped again and turned back. He'd pulled his hood up against the wind.

"Because Uncle Cyrus told me to use my intuition, and my intuition says the information we need is down there."

Straight down. I mean, this section of cliff wasn't actually a sheer drop down to the rocky base leading to the strip of beach, but if I let myself think about it...

"Well," Stefon said, "we might as well go, then. Do you wanna lead?"

My answer to that question was also no, but I nodded yes anyway. Then, stepping as carefully in my clunky hiking boots as I could, I skirted between the rocks, patting the tuft of sea grass with one hand as I went.

Bracing myself against the sloping cliff with my hands—thank goodness I had remembered to wear heavy work gloves and not my usual fingerless wool things—I gently stepped my way down.

My boot slipped, but I caught myself on a rock. Maybe this would be okay. Step-by-step, handhold-by-handhold, I could work my way down the slope, heading toward that scrap of brown cloth.

Stefon's boots sent showers of pebbles and grit down toward me. Maybe having him follow behind was a bad idea. Especially considering how big and bulky he was. If he slipped, I was toast. Too late now.

I found the next foothold and kept going.

I hate this I hate this I hate this. I'd started up a litany inside to keep myself from screaming. It wasn't the most useful idea I'd had, but what can I say? I was running on instinct and my instinct really did hate it.

I tried to do what Uncle Cyrus told me to and expand my peripheral vision. That was supposed to help me pick up on subtle energies and psychic information. But so far, the steady thump of my heart, the pounding of the ocean down below, and the screech of gulls drowned out any information that might have been available.

"Come on," I said to myself. "Get a grip." As the words left my mouth, I reached out to a spindly bush and grabbed on. My boots skidded and I tripped, yanking at the bush to stop myself. It pulled free of the cliffside.

"Holy…"

I tumbled down the hill.

Slamming and scraping, flipping and smacking, hard. Hard. Hard. Gray ocean, brown earth, gray sky… I scrambled to get a toehold, or a handhold, or anything. Anything except this terrifying, gut-wrenching, bruising fall.

Gray. Brown. Gray. Pain.

Stefon's boots hit my shoulder and I yelled. He barreled past, both of us slamming down and down and down again.

Finally, somehow, he stopped just beneath me, and I smacked into his upraised arms, almost sending us both hurtling down again. I felt his knees bend to take the shock, heard him grunt, felt his breath on my face. My own breath. Sobbing.

"Goddess, that hurt."

He just grunted again.

My eyes were streaming and I shook with adrenaline.

"Okay," I panted out. Then cleared my throat and tried again. Louder this time. "We're okay."

"Damn," Stefon replied, then burst out laughing. I joined him. We were both punchy and hysterical. I climbed off his big body and onto the outcropping we'd stopped on.

14

"Where to next?" Stefon asked once we stopped laughing. It was a completely ridiculous situation. And one I wasn't sure how we were going to get out of. I untucked my scarf out from the collar of my coat and wiped the dirt, tears, and sweat off my face.

"I never want to climb down this cliff again."

"I'm with you," Stefon replied. "But unfortunately we're kind of stuck here now. So, which way?"

I fought my breath, trying to slow it down. Trying to calm the beating of my heart.

"Here, let me help." Stefon's arms engulfed me again. He pressed me against the whole, glorious bulk of him, there on that ledge on the windswept cliffside, with the surf pounding relentlessly below.

Immediately, whatever animal nature lived inside me calmed itself down. Even though we were clearly *not* safe, feet above deadly rocks and boulders, wicked tree trunks, and the riptides that killed multiple people every year...even with all of that, for that moment, I felt safe.

Not leaving the circle of his arms, I did what Uncle Cyrus always told me to, and reached with my extra senses. But this time, instead of softening my eyes, I exhaled, and imagined I could soften the edges of my mind. Instead of focusing on one particular thing, I wanted to try to reach out and sense everything around me.

Pebbles, plovers, and insects, small crabs on the beach, the voices of the giant, fallen trees talking to the ancient rocks.

But what was out of place? That was what I was seeking, right? If I saw patterns, what was not part of the pattern? Where were things missing, or snarled, or...?

"Heck if I know," I murmured. I wasn't getting anywhere.

"What?" Stefon asked.

I just shook my head and didn't reply. There had been something by that bush where we fell. That scrap of cloth. But also something else? Maybe footprints, if I hadn't just imagined them. And a glimmering, I realized now.

I exhaled again, then inhaled the cold, salty air. Softened. Reached.

Yes. There were footprints.

I saw them now, clearly, through my psychic eyes. We'd plunged way too far off course.

The adrenaline from the fall had worn off, and I began to shiver. It was dang cold on the cliff face, with the storm clouds gathering again above the ocean down below. There was no red jacket in sight, which was one good thing, I guessed.

"We have to go back up." I pointed.

Stefon just nodded, bless him, as if it was no big deal. Good in a crisis, he was.

"Let's look and see if we can find a pathway," he said.

What a good sport.

I looked up, and the path became clear as well. It was so easy, why couldn't I see it before? It wasn't a *wide* path but it was so clearly a path.

"Let's go," I said, and started up and just to our right.

Stefon kept close, following right behind where I could still hear him. The path wove in and out like a ribbon among the rocks and bushes, heading steadily up and south. I glanced down at my feet and saw something else.

The sandy soil *did* glimmer here. And yep. There were the footprints. Tiny ones. And just beyond the footprints, was the opening of what must be a cave.

I turn my head towards Stefon. "You got my back?"

"Always."

I turned back, took a deep breath, and crouched down.

Then I stuck my head inside the small, dark entrance of the cave.

15

I was falling again, hurtling downward, without the
breath to scream. I was falling through a strange
darkness, flickering with glowing faery lights.

Tumbling end over end, feet overhead and back
again. But when I landed on my back, it was soft as a
cloud, or a pile of the sheepskins Stefon brought on his
medieval camping trips.

I blinked.

And five little square heads stared, blinking back
down at me. And then I heard a voice.

"Sarah?"

I struggled up onto my elbows and the little square
faces backed away. Beyond them was a very familiar
face. Round jaw, mud colored, floppy hair, blue eyes,
and a nose with a slight bend in the middle.

"Toby?"

The hob's face lit up. They were crouched, back
against the earth wall, brown clothing blending into
the surroundings. Toby is not nearly as tall as I am—I

don't think they top four foot ten—but that's still taller than the chaneques, who had plenty of standing room.

"Wow, am I glad you're here," Toby said. "I wasn't sure anyone would even notice we were gone!"

I shook my head, trying to clear it. That sent a sharp spike of pain into my right temple. Nice.

Toby was still talking. "How in the world did you find us? And why did you even know to look?"

I pushed myself all the way up to sitting and bashed my head on the roof of the cave.

"Ouch."

Shucking off my hat, I rubbed at the offended spot. But frankly, this new injury wasn't as bad as all the bumps and bruises I'd sustained falling down the darn cliff face.

"Well, for one thing, Cecilia showed up completely frantic. And for another"—I looked around at the expectant faces of the chaneques—"Mrs. Vargas was worried about you all."

One of them leaned sideways and elbowed another in the rib, then excitedly signed something, as if to say: *I told you she would notice.* At least, that's what it seemed like.

"The real question is," I said, "what the heck are you guys doing here? Why don't you just leave?"

"Well," Toby replied. "That's the problem."

The chaneques signed, as if that would explain everything.

"I don't get it," I said. "What's the problem?"

I looked around, and couldn't see any reason why they wouldn't be able to leave the little cave. Although, come to think of it, the cave looked suspiciously like the one that the chaneques lived in in Mrs. Vargas's restaurant garden.

"Do you not want to leave?"

Toby scratched their head. "It isn't that I don't want to leave," they said. "Or we don't. It's just that it doesn't seem prudent to do so."

I still didn't understand it. There was something really big I was missing, and I didn't think it was just because I was dense, or didn't use my magic, or whatever Uncle Cyrus might say. Something about this whole situation was fishy, and it wasn't just that we were above the ocean.

Speaking of which, the cave was a little claustrophobic. I looked upward, and could just see light coming in through the opening, which was weird, because it felt as if I'd fallen a lot further than that. Looking at it now, I could hear the distant rumble of ocean and see a ledge leading toward the entryway. A ledge that would be really easy to climb.

The rumble increased.

Dammit. That wasn't just the ocean. That was the storm, heading our way again. I really didn't want to be stuck in here.

"Something's going on here." I turned back to Toby and put my hands on my hips. "And don't tell me it's that the chaneques can't climb, because I know they live in caves just like this one."

I looked at the small beings. They looked away.

"I also think the chaneques have a lot of magic, and since that magic is earth magic... Toby. What aren't you all telling me?"

He looked away too.

I leaned closer and sneezed. The cave was really dusty and my movement was kicking it up.

"Toby?" I wiped my nose on my scarf. I really needed to wash the thing when I got back home. If I ever got back home.

More silence, more shuffling from the chaneques as they signed to each other. One of the small beings walked over to Toby, tapped them on the shoulder, and then signed something emphatically.

Toby shook their head.

The chaneque signed again, mouth set in determination. It was clear there was a disagreement.

"I don't think it's a good idea," Toby finally said. The chaneque threw up his hands and turned to me, signing something with short dark fingers.

I shook my head. "I'm sorry. I don't understand your language."

The chaneque turned back to Toby and gave them a look. Toby sighed.

"All right." The hob wiped a streak of dirt across their forehead and looked back at me. It struck me that being in a place filled with dirt must be driving Toby to distraction. Hobs liked nothing more than for everything to be clean and tidy, including themselves.

"The chaneques think I should tell you the truth."

It's about time, I thought, but I didn't say anything. I just waited. I was clearly learning something from Uncle Cyrus, because that was one of his tricks: just remain quiet with a judgmental or expectant look on your face, and eventually your opponent will talk.

"I kidnapped them."

"You what?" I was completely flummoxed. I'd never

really understood what that word meant before, but now I felt it down to my core. Flummoxed. That was me. "But who kidnapped *you*?"

"You don't understand," Toby said. "I did."

I filled with a sudden fury. "Do you know how worried Cecilia is? And Mrs. Vargas? What do you think you're…"

I scrambled to my knees, winced, then crawled to a taller part of the cave where I could stand. My head barely cleared the rough ceiling, but it was better than sitting on my bruises in the dirt.

Toby held up both hands as if to defend themself. "I know. And I'm sorry for that. I know how this must look."

"How this must look?" I swear, the veins must have been bulging in my neck, I was so angry. "I am…I just risked my neck, and Stefon's too, climbing down this dang cliff to save you. We were coming to your dang rescue." Well, not exactly, but Toby didn't need to know that. "And you're telling me you don't need to be rescued? You're telling me you left your girlfriend in the middle of the night without so much as a note?"

Something else was wrong. I looked around a little cave. The chaneques looked right back, square faces placid. It seemed as if now that Toby was talking, the squat chaneques were content.

What else was I missing? Besides the obvious? The obvious was why in the world would a hob steal themself away in the middle of the night and kidnap a bunch of garden spirits?

Besides, I knew Toby: they loved Cecilia with all their heart and would do nothing to hurt her.

At least, not on purpose.

Then another thought pinged the back of my head. The missing question.

"Whose car did you use? Cecilia said your scooter..."

Toby exhaled loudly and rubbed their hands against filthy brown jeans. "There's an old SUV I keep at my uncle's place, for when I need to haul things around or run bigger errands. Cecilia keeps forgetting I have it."

Well, that answered one question, at least.

"Okay, you're all coming with me. Stefon has to be worried about me by now, and this is getting ridiculous."

The chaneques backed up against a wall of the cave, shaking their heads, big eyes wide.

Toby just looked resigned. "I'm telling you, we can't leave."

"And why exactly is that?"

"Because we're all in danger."

16

———

"I definitely need backup for this."

I said the words out loud, but I wasn't really saying them to anyone in the cave. My thoughts were racing, thinking of Uncle Cyrus, who was a phone call away. And the teens, who'd be showing up at the bookstore sometime today. And Stefon, who was probably worried sick outside. I was also thinking of myself. I really wanted to get the heck out of this place. Plus, I had no idea what Toby was talking about.

Or what had happened to Rolf's grandmother.

"In danger from what? Or whom?"

"The rogue witch," they said.

"The rogue witch? What is this, some video game?"

Toby sniffed, clearly offended. "If you bothered to practice your magic and study the old books, you'd know that rogue witches are dangerous."

Way to kick the person who came to help you.

"I don't get it, what rogue witch? And what would a

rogue witch want..." I stopped myself, dirty scarf suddenly tight around my neck.

"With us? What would she want with small, *insignificant* faery creatures? Is that what you were about to say?"

Toby practically bristled with indignation.

"No. That's not what I was saying at all." Which was a big fat lie.

I really needed to get out of this cave. But I needed to calm Toby down first, and get some more information.

"Okay," I said, plopping myself back down on the hard floor. I just couldn't hold myself upright anymore, and was already filthy, so what did it matter? Luckily my butt had plenty of padding. But I winced as some of the bruises I got on the fall made themselves more apparent.

"Just tell me what happened. Why do you think you're in danger? And why are you all hiding in this cave?"

"Someone's after us. We think it's a rogue witch. I started noticing strange things about a month ago, and then when I was eating lunch at the Vargas's place, the chaneques flagged me down. They had been getting signs that trouble was coming. Someone or something had been messing with their gardens. Moving stones and plants. Changing the energy of the place."

"Like they were looking for something, or what?"

Toby shrugged and the chaneques didn't sign anything. So. More information I wasn't getting. Okay.

"So what made you decide to leave in the middle of the night? And why didn't you ask for help?"

Toby hung their head and said, so softly I had to lean forward to catch their words, "You don't know what it's like, being the way we are."

"You're right," I said carefully, "I don't. I don't think anyone can know what's happening with another person, let alone another type of person."

Toby looked up at me then, eyes rimmed with red. "We smaller beings... We just have our homely little magics. And the rest of you—warlocks, witches, and sorcerers—don't really care about us, other than to value what we can do for you. And don't tell me that's not true, I have a lifetime telling me it is."

I didn't have a good reply to that. Toby was probably right. I'd seen how Uncle Cyrus's friends treated even me, a common witch, plus a witch who wasn't using her magic.

"What if we promise to protect you? What if we get you out of here?"

"And what? Hide us somewhere?"

"Look Toby, you can't stay in this cave forever, especially since we don't even know yet what is stalking you, or what the danger looks or feels like."

He shivered then and so did the chaneques.

"Oh," he said darkly, "that's what I've been trying to tell you. We know exactly what it feels like."

"And?"

"It feels like rogue magic. And it feels like death."

"All right then. That does it. I'm getting you out of here. And Stefon is here, willing to help. We're going to figure this out, but we have to figure it out together."

I stood again, brushing off my jeans, which was a

useless endeavor. I turned the chaneques. "What do you think?"

The dark-haired one I was beginning to think of as the leader—if they had such things—turned to the others and signed something. Two of them signed back, and the other two remaining ones just stood, clearly waiting for a decision to be made. I realized I had no idea how their society worked. Maybe Toby was right: all I cared about was that they kept Mrs. Vargas's garden looking pretty.

I cursed myself for not noticing before.

The dark-haired one turned, signed towards me, and then nodded.

I turned back to Toby.

"It looks like they're agreeing?"

Toby nodded.

"Okay then. How, exactly, do we get out of here?"

The dark haired chaneque grinned and rubbed his hands together, and then all of the small garden faery-gnome creatures snapped their fingers three times.

I was hurtling through the air again, but this time I was falling up.

17

─────────

I fell to the ground, smacking my hands hard and bruising my knees. Again.

I was going to be nothing but bruises by the time this whole ordeal was done. As I crouched there, panting, staring at the brown dirt, I realized the earth was damp. It must've started raining while I was inside the cave. And sure enough, along with the shouting of the teens—wait, the teens were here?— and Stefon's voice bellowing somewhere down the cliff, I heard, smelled, and tasted rain. The light sort of rain that Oregonians don't even notice.

It was nice.

Much nicer than falling down a cliff and tumbling into some sort of magicked cave.

My parents were both dead. I was going to live a normal life. That was the plan. The thing I had chosen for myself. I was supposed to just be a bookstore owner. But then Uncle Cyrus... And Toby... And all the rest of it...

Magic. There was no escaping magic.

My mind was wandering. I shook my head to try and clear my thoughts, but that just caused another sharp spike of pain in my right temple.

"Sarah." Uncle Cyrus, sounding worried. His feet scraped near me. Bay Rum. Frankincense. Fancy black wingtips—completely unsuited for an Oregon cliff top—and then his hands were under my armpits, lifting me to a standing position, helped by two other sets of hands. The scent of spearmint gum joined the smell of soft rain on earth. Yep. Teenagers.

"What happened?" Tabitha asked, bouncing annoyingly. "The store wasn't open and we got worried!" Tracy stood at her side, strangely subdued.

"Sarah." Uncle Cyrus spoke again. He placed his hands on my shoulders and looked at me. Rain droplets dotted his face beneath an Irish tweed hat. Uncle Cyrus really needed hats. Being bald and all that.

Huh. Maybe Stefon and I could go to Ireland for vacation some day. Wouldn't that be nice?

Uncle Cyrus flicked his eyes, right to left and back again

"What are you doing?" I asked, shoving at his wool-covered chest. The eye-flicking thing was just weird.

"Making sure your pupils are both the same size."

"Are they?"

He nodded.

Well, that was something at least. I had a splitting headache, but at least I didn't have a concussion. Or not a bad one.

I heard something large scrambling up the hill and turned, looking past Toby who stood, arms wrapped around themself. The chaneques gathered in a clump around the hob, tugging at Toby's pants and jacket, trying to coax them farther away from the edge.

Stefon's head and shoulders crested the top, face as gloomy as the storm clouds that turned from light gray to black as I watched. This wasn't just any rain. A huge storm gathered itself over the ocean. And it seemed too dark to be morning anymore.

Stefon was an angry wreck.

He made it all the way to the top, stumbled, and raced toward me, gripping my shoulders so hard it felt as if he was going to add more bruises to my already abused body.

"What *happened* to you? You were gone for *hours*! Do you know how out of my mind I was? Are you okay?" He was shaking and huffing. He looked up at Cyrus. "Is she okay?"

"Hey," I said, "I'm right here."

And then he folded me into a bone-crushing hug that I happily returned.

"Don't do that again, okay? Whatever it was," he whispered in my ear.

"I'll try not to," I murmured back. But considering I hadn't expected it to happen in the first place, I wasn't sure how I could make good on that promise.

I pulled away and looked past him again. Toby looked small and pale, hair plastered to their head. Why didn't they pull their hood up?

"Toby? You doing all right?"

"I just have the bends."

"What?"

The lead chaneque signed something at me, but I shook my head, signaling that I didn't understand.

Uncle Cyrus stepped forward. "Toby shifted magical states too rapidly just now, before fully recovering from the last round of whatever they and the chaneques have been doing. Am I correct?"

Toby nodded wearily, shuffling closer, feet dragging.

"Let's get off this clifftop before that storm hits," Cyrus said behind me. "We'll reconvene at your home, Sarah, once everyone who needs to has the chance to dry off. We'll bring food, and talk about this there. Toby? Is the car you used around somewhere, and do you feel up to driving?"

Toby ran a hand over their face. "Yeah. I'm good to drive. My car is just up the way, after the curve." They gestured toward the highway. "I'll bring the chaneques and let Mrs. Vargas know."

We still hadn't found Rolf's grandmother, but in the moment, I was too tired and filthy to dwell on the fact, so I pocketed that worry at least until I'd had a shower.

"Thank you," Uncle Cyrus said, then turned to the teenagers. "You two can ride with me."

And then, as if realizing something, Cyrus looked at Stefon. "Can you get her home okay?"

"I'm right here," I said again.

Uncle Cyrus flicked his eyes toward me, then back to Stefon.

"Yes sir," Stefon replied.

"Yes *sir*?" I couldn't believe it. When the heck did he start calling Uncle Cyrus sir? I didn't know if it was some sort of chivalry thing, or a cis man thing, or what, but suddenly, I was too tired to figure it out. All I knew was, sometimes when Stefon got all knightly and bossy, it was kind of hot. But today? Today had been too scary for any part of it to be sexy. So I settled on feeling mildly annoyed.

Ignoring both of them, I followed Toby and the garden fairies and started walking back towards the road. We had found a small place to park about ten yards back up the highway, probably where Toby had left their vehicle.

I looked back over my shoulder.

"You coming?"

Stefon shook his head, but followed me anyway. My knight in grubby jeans and hoodie.

I couldn't even stop to appreciate him. I just wanted to get home.

I'd lost enough time for one day, and apparently hadn't eaten a darn thing since my cereal at breakfast.

18

By the time we swung by Stefon's for him to grab clean clothes, and then both took showers at my place—separately, thank you; we were both still a little mad at each other—Uncle Cyrus and the teens had come back bearing snacks, which is what happens when you put teens in charge of dinner, I guessed. Mrs. Vargas, Toby, and Cecilia arrived after that, and then the storm hit full force.

Rain lashed at the windows, the trees shook, and thunder rumbled in the distance. Every lamp in my snug home was lit to drive away the cold night.

We were all crowded into my little cottage living room. I had lit a fire in the green tiled Craftsman hearth, and sat next to Stefon on the navy sofa, with Mrs. Vargas to my left clutching a rust-colored throw pillow, for comfort, I guess. Uncle Cyrus was in my dad's comfy reading chair, looking elegant as always. The two teens dragged out chairs from my kitchen table. They both had plates of food on their laps, but it was clear that Mrs. Vargas and Uncle Cyrus didn't feel like eating. I didn't either, though I nibbled on a piece of Swiss cheese before popping a cracker into my mouth. I was eating more for something to do than because I wanted food.

My hunger had disappeared into the knot of worry in my gut.

Cecilia and Toby sat on poofs on the floor next to the fireplace. Toby was inhaling food as if they hadn't eaten in days, and maybe they hadn't. Cecilia sat, legs crossed, ignoring the food on the rectangular wood coffee table. She cradled a mug of tea, and every so often, would reach out and pet Toby's seal-dark hair.

"Are the chaneques safe?" I asked.

Mrs. Vargas nodded. "Your uncle, he said they would be safe in his garden."

"His garden?"

Uncle Cyrus didn't have a garden as far as I knew. He traveled too much. Cyrus gazed into the flames as if we weren't talking about him, or as if what we were saying was beneath notice. That just increased my irritation.

"Would someone care to explain?" I asked.

Stefon looked up from his food, startled. Leaning forward, he grabbed a glass full of soda before settling back into the sofa.

"What are you talking about?" Stefon asked.

Was no one paying attention? Lightning flashed through the curtains and thunder cracked almost immediately. Dang.

I turned to Stefon. "As far as I know, Uncle Cyrus here doesn't have a garden, but Mrs. Vargas says her spirits are there."

"Not my spirits." She coughed, waving a hand in front of her face. "Not even Mr. Vargas can lay claim to that. No, our garden belongs to the chaneques. The chaneques do not belong to our garden."

I looked at Uncle Cyrus, who was finally paying attention, though pretending not to. He crossed his legs and picked a piece of nonexistent lint from yet another merino wool sweater. It was lavender this time. If I stopped to wonder how many expensive sweaters he had, the excess would just irritate me more, so I didn't.

"I bought a home in Portland," he said. "On the west side of the river. I thought it would be nice to have a home base closer to you. And it was simple enough to transport the chaneques through a portal to my place there. That short a distance was easy, with their magics combined with mine."

I shook my head. "We will have to talk about your new home later," I said. And about combining the strength of various magical beings. That was some serious magic. "But you're sure that they're safe?"

He leveled his gaze at me. "If you had been keeping up with your studies, you would know that setting up wards and protections is the first thing any witch, warlock, or magician does upon occupying a domicile. My home and garden are all very securely warded, I can assure you. Nothing unfriendly or unknown will be able to cross my threshold."

I looked around my house, suddenly worried.

"Your father's wards are strong enough for now," Uncle Cyrus said, in answer to my swiveling head. "At their base are the original wards your mother set, and your father reinforced them every year."

"But he's been gone for...," I said, throat constricting, all of a sudden wishing I had a glass of wine instead of the tea mug that was sitting on the coffee table waiting for me, rapidly growing cool.

"I took over feeding the protections once it became clear you needed a break," Cyrus said, voice gentle.

The words he didn't speak were loud and clear, though. They were the ones he'd been saying ever since he rudely popped into The Widening Gyre. It was about time I took up the mantle again. Dammit. My obliviousness to the wards were one more sign that I'd been shirking my magic duties.

"I still don't get it," Tracy said around a half-chewed stack of salami and crackers. She swallowed. "What did you think was after you?"

Toby grunted and swallowed their own food before speaking from behind the floppy curtain of mud brown bangs, staring at the coffee table instead of addressing Tracy directly.

"Something's been following me for the past three months. And the chaneques said that something bad had been in their garden, and tried to get past the protections at the grotto."

"So you decided you needed to leave?" I asked

"Without telling anyone?" Cecilia asked. There was pain tinged with anger in her voice, but I could tell she was trying to not get into it with Toby. That was good. Toby didn't look as if they could take the conflict right now, and we didn't really have time to hash any of this stuff out.

Toby shrugged. "Didn't want to put anyone else in danger. Besides, we couldn't tell what or who it was so we didn't see how anyone could investigate."

"Toby..." Cecilia sighed.

"I know," they replied. "It wasn't the smartest thing I've ever done. But I just panicked."

Cecilia threw an arm around their skinny shoulder and pulled Toby closer. "We're in this together, got that?"

Toby nodded.

Stefon nudged my thigh with his own, as if to say, *Yeah, got that?* I pressed back. Message received.

"So what do we do now?" Tabitha asked.

Everyone looked at me.

I took a breath, long and slow, then exhaled. Trying to buy myself some time.

I wanted nothing more than to look to Uncle Cyrus, but I knew he would refuse to take the lead. Everyone had come to me because this was on me. Stefon was right.

I needed to see the pattern.

"We need to find out who else has been affected," I said. "We need to fire up the magic network and ask the other hobs, brownies, and gnomes, and all the rest if they've felt or seen anything unusual lately. And I can ask around town some more, too. So far, Angie said her greenhouses had been messed with. And I checked with Delta Crabbit, whose family owns the tree farm. She didn't seem to know anything."

The jury was out on Ms. Crabbit, though. Something was still going on with her.

"I can do any computer work you need," Stefon said. "Cyrus? Maybe you could get with me and Toby and tell me what I need to do to look."

"We can go around tomorrow with my mom and talk to more people if that helps," Tracy said.

I nodded. "You two should stick to research. I mean, sure, if you're out somewhere, mention that you've heard some people's gardens have been tampered with, but I don't want you doing any more than that."

Tracy gave me one of those *whatever* looks, but I just stared back. There was no way I was sending those teens into possible danger.

"But what are you going to do?" Tabitha asked.

I was going to ask around town, but held my tongue on that.

"Tonight, while I have all of you here? We're going to clear all this food back to the kitchen and set up for ritual."

I needed to do some scrying.

"Cool!" Tracy said and leapt up. She and Tabitha both started scurrying around, clattering dishes and stacking food, bringing everything to the kitchen. I smiled. Maybe having teenagers around was a good thing.

It made me think back to when I was their age. I was serious, like Tabitha, but still had the energy of Tracy.

Those were good days, despite my mother being taken away from me. There was still magic in the air, until, in my pain, I began to push it all away.

It was time to get more of that magic back.

If my destiny was to see patterns and to help people?

I was going to see what I could do.

While everyone cleaned up, I went to my bedroom, plugged my phone into a speaker, and Stevie Nicks's voice filled the room, singing about poetry and drowning in the sea of love. It was a song my father sang to me all the time when I was little. He used to tell me that I was named for that song, even though they spelled my name differently.

And even though I was their beloved child and not the source of heartbreak that almost broke up the band.

Then, on my bruised and battered knees, I dug into the big closet. Singing along with Stevie, I shoved aside boots and shoes and a couple of fallen scarves.

This particular song was to me what a pot of macaroni and cheese was to someone else: comfort food. It brought both of my parents back to me for the few minutes that Fleetwood Mac sang and played.

"What are you looking for, babe?"

I hadn't heard Stefon come in. Whatever noise he'd

made was drowned out by my warbling, and the song currently on repeat. But I had found what I was looking for. A handmade wooden jewelry box with a false bottom.

My mother's magic box. It used to hold pride of place in my father's bedroom, but I put it away when he got sick.

I couldn't stand to think of losing her and him at the same time. It was easier to act as if she was just a distant memory instead of an active presence in Dad's life. It hurt too much, his love for her.

Just like my love for him hurt. But it was time to change that now, too.

I backed out of the closet and levered myself up to my feet, the smallish, heavy box cradled in my arms.

I wiped a thin film of dust from the box with my sweatshirt sleeve and carefully set it on top of my dresser.

"I was looking for this."

Stefon came to stand beside me, but he didn't touch me and he didn't speak. I could feel him all the same, radiating warmth the way he always did. I stretched my toes out in my sheepskin-lined slippers, planting myself as firmly on the floor as I could. Then, fingers lightly touching the dark wood, I lifted the lid. There was a shallow box set just beneath the lid, which held my mother's ritual jewelry. Silver. Amethyst. Moonstone.

But that wasn't what I was looking for. I carefully lifted out the box tray and beneath it, set in a padded depression in the purple velvet above what I knew was a false bottom, lay her crystal ball.

"Wow," Stefon whistled. "That was your mom's?"

I nodded, not trusting myself to speak. Sitting next to the ball was a small silver ring stand with three feet. Carved on each foot were the three phases of the moon: crescent, full, and half. I lifted out the stand and set it on my dresser top and then cradled the heavy ball. It was cool to the touch and heavy enough that it took both my palms spread open to lift it from the box and set it was carefully on its stand.

"It's beautiful," Stefon murmured. "How old do you think it is?"

I wiped my hands on my jeans. "You know, I never thought to ask. Dad would've known. But crystals are old, right?"

But it was too late to ask him, wasn't it? "Maybe Uncle Cyrus knows."

My brain skittered past the thought that Uncle Cyrus knew a lot of things, and I wasn't sure whether or not I wanted the information.

We stood there together, breathing quietly. Stefon lightly brushed the back of his hand against mine and I slipped my fingers into his warm palm.

We both just stared down at the crystal orb. Parts of it were cloudy, almost milky; other parts were crystal clear. There were veins and cracks—I guess they were called striations—in the middle of it. I was overcome with an overwhelming urge to bend down and rest my cheek against the crystal. Fall into its depths.

I touched my ear to the cool curve of it.

I could almost hear my mother's voice, whispering to me from the clouds. But really, I heard her voice inside my heart.

Sarah, beautiful one, magic is your gift to the world. Never forget it.

She said that to me three weeks before she died. Back when I still thought I had years of life with her.

Back before she was stolen away.

20

—————

Candles flickered on every available surface. The fire cracked and hissed every time a splat of rain made its way down the chimney. Someone must have dropped some resins onto the logs when I was in the bedroom because the air was perfumed with that "Warlock High Church" smell. In other words, the room smelled a lot like my uncle if he also wore burning birch and pine perfume.

Some people think warlocks are just male witches, but that isn't the case. All sorts of genders can be witches, warlocks, sorcerers, or magicians. It all has to do with the flavor of the magic, and the person's natural abilities and training. Sorcerers worked mostly in the ætheric realms, witches with the natural elements, and warlocks? Well, they had nifty cool space and time shifting abilities, along with their elemental magic. They also tended to like ritual even more than witches. And magicians? They liked high ritual the most, and all their magic stemmed from that, rather than an innate connection to the elemental forces.

Cyrus was some combination of warlock and magician, with a little sorcery thrown into the mix. He'd been practicing for decades, and collected magical techniques like a corvid collects shiny objects.

See what you could do if you only practiced more? I shoved the thought aside. I was about to scry, wasn't I?

The storm had not abated; as a matter of fact, it seemed that its power had only grown.

I wiped my hands on my jeans and shucked my hoodie. With all the people, the candles, and the fire, I was suddenly way too hot. My sheepskin-lined slippers had to go, too.

Stefon appeared at my side, offering a clear tumbler of water. I drank half of it in one go, relishing the coolness of it.

But it did nothing to quench the fire lit in my belly, mind, and heart.

The Sacred Fire, the ancient bards had called it. All the best poets had it. And apparently, sometimes witches, too. I didn't know what it meant, but it seemed that the elements had listened to my internal decision to reclaim my powers, and they'd rolled in with the storm.

"Are you ready?" Uncle Cyrus's voice was calm and clear, and soothed the parts of me that were still panicking.

"I'm ready," I replied, surprised to find my own voice was steady, too.

I sat on a pouf this time, in front of the coffee table. The low wooden rectangle had been transformed into an altar. A purple paisley shawl covered it. Two tapers gleamed in glass candlesticks, set just behind and to the sides of my mother's crystal ball. The light glimmered on the surface, but the underside was still in shadow, just the way Uncle Cyrus said it should be.

Mrs. Vargas sat across from me, on the couch next to my uncle. Davíd was minding the restaurant, I guessed.

Stefon stood guard at the front door, sword in hand. I guess that had been in the trunk of his car, which seemed like a foolish thing. What if he'd gotten pulled over and searched? I guess we'd have that conversation later.

In the moment, I was glad to see him standing there, back straight, bare feet planted, sword and dark eyes dancing with the candle flames.

"Try to relax." Uncle Cyrus's voice was soothing. "Follow your breath. Let everything slow down inside. Allow yourself to open to the vision."

I tried, straightening my spine, and focusing on my breathing. The taste of salty ocean spray mixed with burnt sugar in my mouth. I fought down the urge to drink more water.

Maybe this was why I never liked salted caramel. It reminded me too much of the taste of magic.

You need to focus, Sarah, I said to myself. I rolled my neck and shoulders, shook out my hands, exhaled, and tried again.

I let my fingertips trace the crystal orb again. It was still cool, but this time it gave a little zap, as if to let me know it was paying attention. Or maybe it was telling me *I* needed to pay attention.

I lifted my fingers, set my hands lightly on the coffee table to either side of the crystal ball, and leaned forward, trying not to stare, trying not to focus.

I was trying to simply *be* with the quartz sphere, the way my dad and Uncle Cyrus tried to teach me. They insisted that this skill—was it a skill? I wasn't sure— was important for every type of magic, but especially the divinatory arts like Tarot or scrying.

Sounds and images and tastes and sensations all swirled around and through me. It was as if the crystal ball was doing its best to reach me in any way it could. I inhaled, and exhaled, and tried to relax some more.

And then I saw a gray shadow in the shape of a small woman, it looked like. She was standing on the cliff top—I could hear waves crashing beneath her. She raised her hands.

She called the storm.

"But what does this have to do with Toby and the others?"

"What did she say?" I heard Tabitha whisper. I ignored her. I hadn't meant to speak the words out loud.

The woman swayed and jerked. Outside my cottage, thunder crashed.

In my vision, I saw a lightning flash. It turned the sky purple, and illuminated the figure standing there. It definitely looked like a woman to me, with long dark hair shot through with gray. The winds whipped her hair around. She tilted back her head and laughed.

Her hair reminded me of the Goddess woman in the Blueberry Café, but I couldn't be sure.

"Who are you?" I whispered.

She turned to look my way. I peered through the storm, trying to catch a glimpse of her face.

My phone buzzed and rang somewhere in the room, snapping me out of the vision, flinging me back into my body, rocking me on the pouf. My back hit the soft cushions of the sofa seat, my hands flew to my face, and I opened my eyes.

"What's happening to her?" Stefon's voice was an urgent growl. But he had not left his post.

Cyrus crouched down next to me. "What happened? What did you see?"

"It looked like a woman. Long dark hair. Straight. Silvered with gray."

"And her face?"

I shook my head. Tabitha handed me a fresh cup of tea.

"Thanks." I wrapped my hands around the heavy mug, grateful for the warmth. I hadn't realized it, but I was shivering.

I raise the cup and inhaled. Spearmint.

"Right as she turned to look at me," I said, "the phone rang and then I snapped back, out of the vision. Should I try again?"

"What do you mean, she turned to look at you?" Cyrus's voice was sharp.

I took a tiny sip of tea, testing to see if it was cool enough to drink. It was, just barely. I was still shaking, and really wishing for my slippers and hoodie back.

"It was almost as if she knew I was there and wanted to see who I was."

"That's not good, right?" Stefon's voice again.

Cyrus rocked back on his heels and then stood.

"I'm not certain," he said. "But I also think we're done for right now. You can shut down the extra protections."

From behind me, I felt Stefon *do* something, which was strange, because as far as I knew, he had no magic. But maybe being a warrior was a type of magic all its own.

And then he was back in the room. Sheathing his sword, he slid it carefully beneath the couch, then sat and pulled me up next to him. It didn't take much convincing to get me off that pouf. I cuddled up next to him, his warmth radiating outward like a fire. Yeah. I really did love him.

He felt like home.

That was still a big shift in my mindset, but I didn't have time to think about it.

Cyrus sat back down in his chair, tapping his chin. I just sat, and so did everyone else. Cecilia and Toby sat with their arms around each other, and the two teens were quiet in their chairs, not even bouncing.

That in itself was magical.

"What are you thinking?" Stefon asked.

Cyrus stared into the flames. "I'm thinking the description sounds an awful lot like Thekla."

A vague memory shifted and stirred inside me, but I couldn't quite place it.

"Who is Thekla?" Tabitha asked.

"A very powerful sorcerer."

"The rogue... But what does she want with us?" Toby asked.

"I have no idea," Uncle Cyrus replied. "Though I have my suspicions."

My uncle turned hooded eyes on me. "You're twenty-eight?"

"Yes." What a strange question. He knew exactly how old I was. "What does that have to do with anything?"

"Give me some time," he replied.

Well, wasn't that great. He'd turned all enigmatic on me. I had no idea who this Thekla was and what my age had to do with anything; all I knew was that my magic was back, full force.

Now I just had to figure out what to do with it.

21

There was both a missed call and a text.

"It's Davíd," I said. "Did he call you too?"

Mrs. Vargas pulled her phone out of her purse. "Yes, he did. I set my phone to silent before you began. His text says it is important. Would you call, mija? I don't trust myself right now."

I nodded and hit dial. The phone rang and rang but he didn't pick up. There was a pounding on the door, and Stefon leapt up to answer.

I ended the call and heard Stefon greet someone, and then the thumping of boots and the rustle of a jacket being removed.

Davíd followed Stefon back into the living room.

"Mijo!" Mrs. Vargas rose to hug her son. "What has happened?"

Davíd looked terrible.

"Do you need something, man?" Stefon asked.

Tabitha and Tracy both leapt up.

"We can get you tea. Or soda?" Tracy said.

David waved his hands and shook his head.

"Have a seat, man." Stefon dragged another chair out from my dining room. David sat heavily and swiped a hand over his rain-wet face.

"Tracy? Would you get David a towel? There's a small closet right next to the bathroom down the hall. And Tabitha? Please take his jacket and hang it by the door."

Team teen was clearly happy to have something to do.

Both were back in a flash, and David nodded gratefully at the towel and wiped himself down.

"Dad called," he said, looking at his mother. "At one of his jobs today, the homeowner asked if he had noticed anything strange up the hill from their house."

My stomach sank. Whatever he was about to tell us seemed like it was very bad.

"And?" Uncle Cyrus said, leaning forward in his chair.

The room was suddenly too warm again, but I forced myself to sit still. I noticed that Stefon still stood, as if he couldn't bear to not be ready to leap into motion at whatever the news was.

"And?" Tabitha repeated Cyrus's question.

In front of me, the crystal ball swirled, as if another vision was trying to come through. I kept splitting my attention between the ball and David's face. The sense of dread increased.

"Dad said there was something very wrong. The land didn't look right. So he went to investigate...."

His mother leaned forward this time. "Davíd. Mijo. Just tell us what is wrong, you are scaring us."

Davíd swallowed. "He found a dead dryad."

I shivered. Cold. Stefon must've felt the same way, because he finally sat down beside me and put an arm around my shoulders, tugging me close.

"You mean dryads are real?" Tabitha asked. We all just looked at her, and she shrugged. "Sorry. I just…"

"It's okay," Stefon said. "This is all pretty new to me, too."

It was, I realized, despite him dating a witch. Oh, he'd told me that he'd seen plenty of freaky things before we even started going out, but encountering uncanny things, and actually believing in a wide variety of magical creatures? It was a bit of a leap, even for nerds who wanted to believe in that sort of thing.

Most people just pretended not to see or hear the weird stuff. It was how the mind protected itself.

"Please," Uncle Cyrus said, "continue, Davíd. And girls, if you wouldn't mind, I think we could all use some tea right about now, or better yet…how about some hot chocolate?"

I knew what he was doing: he was getting them out of the immediate conversation and it was probably a good idea. The teens seemed suspicious, but complied.

"Davíd?" I asked. "What about the dryad?"

He swallowed again and rubbed his hands against his jeans, though they had to still be damp from the rain. I should've told him to sit closer to the fire.

"He said…oh Gods." His bronze face went pale, and he lurched to his feet and raced down my hallway. I heard the bathroom door fly open, slamming against the wall. Soon, the sounds of retching filled the cottage.

Stefon patted my leg. "I'll go check on him."

"Thank you." I stood with him, and headed to the kitchen to make sure the teens were doing all right.

"Did you find everything?" Water boiled in the electric kettle and a big cylinder of instant hot chocolate sat on the counter, which was just as well. Hot chocolate stirred carefully on the stove with some kind of milk is better, but none of us had the energy for making it right now.

"Yeah," Tracy said, "we're okay." Her eyes looked worried, though, and her blond hair was still flat on one side from her jacket hood. She got some mugs down from the cupboard.

"Is Davíd okay, though?" Tabitha asked. "We heard him puking."

She looked a bit steadier than Tracy, at least, and began spooning cocoa mix into the mugs as soon as Tracy set them down.

I shook my head. "To be honest, I'm not sure."

"Sounds pretty bad, what his dad saw," Tabitha said. Tracy poured water over the powder and Tabitha stirred. Once the mugs were ready, I helped them carry the drinks back out to the living room just as Stefon and Davíd arrived again.

After handing around the mugs, we all sat back down. Davíd clutched at his as if it was a lifeline, and I couldn't blame him because I was doing the same.

"You don't have to describe it," Uncle Cyrus said.

"Thanks," Davíd replied. "It sounded horrible. My dad stayed there to try to deal with it."

"Should we go join him?" Stefon asked, staring toward the curtained windows. I knew he was imagining Mr. Vargas on the hillside in the howling storm.

"Does he need help?" Uncle Cyrus asked. Magical help, he meant, and I knew the answer to that.

I looked at my uncle.

"What?" Stefon asked, thunking his hot chocolate down on the altar cloth.

"If this turns out to be murder, Sarah is the closest thing Seashell Cove has to a magical detective," Cyrus said, voice dry.

"And Uncle Cyrus is the closest thing we have to a judge."

It felt as if a bell tolled, deep inside of me. *That* was what I'd been avoiding. No way was I equipped to stand in judgement on any other being's life. I could barely balance my books, let alone the scales of justice. But being a Justice ran in my family, didn't it? It was part of our magic, and I knew that, but had buried the information deep inside.

"Well, damn," Stefon replied.

I had to agree with the sentiment. Taking on that part of Dad's legacy was the last thing I ever wanted to do, but here it was, standing in front of me, staring me down.

"Babe..." Stefon said.

"I don't really have a choice," I replied.

"You always have a choice," Uncle Cyrus replied. His voice was firm, and his eyes flashed fiercely.

But I didn't. Not if I wanted to live with myself.

I turned. "Uncle Cyrus, I think I've just found out

the real reason why I've been avoiding my magic. It's all…" I waved a hand. "This Justice stuff."

"I don't blame you," he said. And I saw that he really didn't. Somehow, the fact that he understood made me feel a little better.

Stefon squeezed my hand. "You don't have to do this alone. Neither of you. I know you think I'm just a pretend knight, but I'm serious about the principles. I'm here for whatever you need."

"Yeah, us too," Tabitha said. "The being here for you part."

Tracy nodded.

"Well," I replied, "there's not much use going out in this storm, but whoever can, let's reconvene here in the morning and head up the hill. Will your dad be able to lead us there?"

David swallowed his hot chocolate and nodded. "Yes. I'll be there too."

Uncle Cyrus stood and carried his mug into the kitchen. The teens followed suit and gathered up everyone else's cups. The party was over, which was good, because I suddenly felt exhausted.

Soon, everyone was putting on coats and boots. Uncle Cyrus was preparing to drive the teens home. I hugged Mrs. Vargas, who felt fragile beneath my hands. Then I hugged David, too.

I looked into his eyes. "Tell your dad we'll find who did this."

Everyone trooped out into the dark and wet, and then Stefon and I were alone, with just the crackling of the fire and the beating of the storm outside the windows.

"How are you going to find out who did this, babe?"

"I have no idea. All I know is I need to."

Because whoever had done this? That person had put my friends in danger and had seriously pissed me off.

22

T he place should've been beautiful.

It was a high, windswept promontory with a view of the ocean to the west and forest to the north. Looking down the slope, I could see the rooftops and the waving flags and banners of the shops on Main Street. I could just make out the big T-Rex skull flag waving outside the fossil shop.

You could practically see the whole town of Seashell Cove from up here.

Once upon a time, this hill was a good spot. A happy spot. Now, just being up here made me feel slightly ill.

Mr. Vargas rubbed his hands against the cold. He looked a bit like a taller, human version of a chaneque. Solidly built, with powerful hands and shoulders, and mud-splattered work boots and jeans underneath, with blue-and-green-plaid flannel under a battered green hooded rain jacket. I wore my own rain jacket, like we all did. I had thought about wearing my bright red one because I needed cheering up, but before we left the house my hand had stayed itself, hovering over the bright jacket before choosing the sober navy, instead. It seemed more respectful somehow, though with the dryad being dead, I didn't think she would care.

Signs of mourning were always for those left behind though, weren't they?

David cleared his throat. "Show us?"

Mr. Vargas grunted and turned, leading the way down a short path into a stand of trees. He had barely spoken since we arrived, but then he never did talk much. He left that for his wife and his son.

I suppose that was why they ran the family restaurant, and he had a gardening business.

Mr. Vargas spoke through his hands, and talented hands they were. They shifted soil and plants and rocks, forming them into new, more pleasing arrangements. And everything he touched seemed to grow. That was his magic. Just like Mrs. Vargas's magic was with food, and David's was with people.

The ground sloped, uneven beneath my boots, but at least once we reached the trees the temperature rose slightly, sheltering us from a breeze I hadn't really even noticed out in the open. I could feel the warm comforting bulk of Stefon behind me. We had convinced the teenagers to not come, saying that too many people tromping around a crime scene wouldn't have been good.

I left them in the closed bookstore with a pile of reference materials to go through, which seemed to placate them. Not that research would do any good, but you never knew.

I'd also called Duncan, who was happy to cut short his winter break and come in to open. He said he was bored anyway, and had just been cleaning house.

That was good, because, though it was still early, I had no idea how long we'd be here on the hillside.

My boots slipped on the mud, and I threw my arms out to catch my balance. By the time I looked up again, father and son had stopped.

I shivered with a cold that had little to do with the temperature.

Mr. Vargas stood at the base of a tall spruce. But where the branches should have been a deep, healthy green, they were mottled brown and white. And just beyond the tree, what used to be a small, spring-fed pond was now a choked-off garbage dump.

How had things changed so quickly?

"Damn," Stefon said, moving past me toward Mr. Vargas.

A sick miasma coated the air, making my tongue taste as if I just swallowed over-steeped tea followed by a rotten banana.

"This is is really bad," Stefon muttered. That was the understatement of the year, and it was clear it didn't take a witch or any other kind of magic person to figure out that things were very wrong.

Mr. Vargas looked heartbroken and sick, and I couldn't blame him. I felt the same.

"What can we do?" I had to ask the question even though I didn't really want to hear the answer.

Mr. Vargas shook his head. "I don't think I can help the tree, but we can come back with garbage bags and clear out the spring."

"And the rest of it?" David looked around, clearly queasy, looking almost as sick as his father did.

"The rest of it," Mr. Vargas replied, "I will do what I can to save. But with the dryad dead, I do not have much hope."

"So the dryad," Stefon asked, "it lived in the tree?"

Mr. Vargas scratched his hair beneath his dark wool cap tucked under his jacket hood. "That is one way of putting it. But it would be more accurate to say that the dryad *was* the tree."

"So killing the dryad would kill the tree?"

"And the other way around. There are accidental deaths, of course. But this?" Mr. Vargas waved a hand, looking as forlorn as I'd ever seen him.

"I'll find out who did this," I pledged. "And you let me know if you find out anything more."

Mr. Vargas nodded, as if satisfied.

"You do that, Sarah. It is a necessary thing."

"How are you going to do that, babe?" Stefon asked.

"I'll figure it out, somehow." I had to. As Mr. Vargas said, this was no accident. The dryad didn't die of natural causes. It was murder, for sure.

If nothing else, I would enlist Cyrus. If he had come back to bug me, he might as well get put to work.

But the fact that he might know who the person in my vision was? I was growing suspicious that Uncle Cyrus might have not come back for me after all. What if he knew more than he was telling me?

23

Stefon dropped me down the hill and then went back to his place to get some work done. My plan was to ask around at a few of the local shops—do some reconnaissance, so to speak—and then go spell Duncan at The Widening Gyre. I should also check in on the teens and see if they had actually discovered anything in the shelves.

I walked down Main Street, past the cheerfully lighted shops beneath the slate-gray sky. The bright banners snapped forlornly, calling out to customers who had all gone home to their dry houses further inland.

I walked towards the fossil store, the one with the T-Rex skull on its banner. Ancient Treasures was its name.

I really liked the owner. Tetris was a cool dude named for some old computer game and just happened to really like fossils.

I pulled open the heavy glass door, and a roaring

noise greeted me. I never knew if it was supposed to be the T-Rex or what, but it had taken a while for it to not startle me. I have heard many a tourist shriek upon entry and then dissolve in laughter.

"Sarah, what brings you here on a work day?" Tetris was an aging white guy with long gray hair pulled back into a ponytail. He wore a faded-to-gray T-shirt with a grinning skull emblazoned on the front. His also gray jeans had a rip in one knee, and complemented his burgundy Doc Martin boots.

"I just needed to check in," I said, looking around. There were big wood and glass cases everywhere. The one nearest me was filled with ammonites, which are my favorites. When I looked up from the case, Tetris was giving me one of his *I may be an old punk rock gamer dude, but that also means I wasn't born yesterday* looks.

"Now Sarah, you know better than to prevaricate with me."

"Fair enough," I replied, then wound my way through the display cases to the counter where he stood, arms crossed in front of that grinning skull on his chest.

"I need your help," I said.

"You know you have it," he replied. "Whatever you want or need, if I can, I'll show up. That's what neighbors do."

And that was why I had come here first, because I believed him. Because to Tetris, everyone was his neighbor.

I never asked what his religion was, and I don't think it mattered. Maybe it was his old punk rock *help your friend up from the floor of the mosh pit* ethic, or maybe it was something else. But he was a good guy, no matter what.

And he did have a little shiny magic about him; I assumed it was from some ancestor a generation or two back.

"Does this conversation need a cup of tea?" he asked.

I would have loved to sit in this shop, surrounded by fossils and bones, listening to the rain and talking to Tetris, but I shook my head no.

"Thanks, but I can't stay long. I just was wondering if you had noticed anything out of the ordinary lately."

He snorted. "Out of the ordinary for Seashell Cove? Or out of the ordinary for someplace ordinary?"

I answered his grin with one of my own. "Out of the ordinary for Seashell Cove."

He pulled up a wooden stool and plopped his skinny butt down. "Now that you mention it, a couple of the regulars have been acting a little bit strange. Stranger than usual, I mean."

"Like who?"

"Crabbit, for one. I mean she's always slightly off, but she seems more agitated these days."

"And?"

"And I've seen a woman out on the cliffs that isn't a local. Never seen her before." Tetris worked his mouth as if he tasted something bad, had swallowed some vinegar.

Everything inside of me went on high alert. "What did she look like?"

"Long, dark, silver-shot hair. Acting like a sorcerer

or witch, which is why I thought it was so strange that I didn't recognize her."

Thekla, I thought. The warlock person Uncle Cyrus talked about.

"You sure she's not just a Goddess worshipper, doing, you know, Goddess worshipper things? I saw a woman like that hanging up fliers down at Angie's."

He frowned. "Could be, now that you've mentioned it. I've seen those types during the summer sometimes, come out to light candles and such. Yeah. That's probably it. Simplest explanation, and all."

We both stared at the fossils for a moment. I know I was thinking out-of-town Goddess worshippers didn't usually come out to the cliff tops alone during the worst of the winter storms.

"And how about you?" He volleyed the question back.

"I also noticed that Ms. Crabbit was acting a little strange, and...I don't know if you heard about it, but up on the lookout? Above town? The big spruce is dead, and the pond is filled with garbage."

He gave a long, low whistle at that.

"That is bad," he said.

And then fell silent.

I didn't blame him. Sometimes there wasn't much more to say.

24

After I left the fossil shop, I decided to walk down half a block, back to the Blueberry Pie Café. I could use some fortification and should check back in with Angie about her greenhouse and to see if she knew anything about the woman tacking up fliers.

Or about dryads.

As I walked down the sidewalk, my phone buzzed in my pocket with an actual phone call. I drew it out. Stefon.

"Hey handsome, I thought you were going to try to get some work done."

"I was," he said, "but then Rolf called."

The hair stood up on the back of my neck.

"And?"

"His grandmother came back."

"Well, that's good news," I said, which didn't explain the stiffness of his tone of voice or the fact that I still felt freaked out by the call. Witch's intuition. Even at my lowest points that was a thing I'd learned to always trust.

"It's not good news. I mean, sure it's good news she's back, but..."

"Stefon..."

"I think I need to come get you. You need to hear what Rolf has to say in person."

"Meet me at The Widening Gyre."

Ending the call, I reversed direction and hoofed it back to my store. I opened the door and wiped my feet on the big mat. The scent of books and the sound of Duncan's favorite bluegrass soothed me. Too bad that wouldn't last.

"Hey boss." Duncan, wearing a Jane Austen portrait T-shirt beneath a vintage, mustard yellow cardigan, flashed me a smile and shoved his black framed glasses higher on his winter-pale nose. His stocky frame perched on the high stool behind the counter, pricing that pile of books I'd left. Duncan was doing me a favor coming in when he should be off. The fact that he was also a great worker and good with customers was a bonus.

A small business owner couldn't ask for anything better. Except, maybe, triple the customers.

"Are the teenagers still here?"

He nodded. "Yeah. Some blond woman came and took them out to lunch and then dropped them back here."

"That's Tracy's mother."

"Where did you pick them up?"

He spoke as if he was talking about a couple of stray cats.

"They just showed up," I said.

"Ain't that the way?" he said. And speaking of cats, Rhiannon walked toward me, and then bounced, all four paws levitating, before bounding toward the back. Duncan gave me a look.

"I think you better follow her. She's been acting squirrelly all day, but I haven't had time to pay much attention."

"Will do."

I wandered through the bookshelves, running my fingers along the spines, pausing occasionally to right a book that had fallen on its side. Some of the shelves looked sparse after the holidays. That would make inventory simpler, at least.

A cold draft sped past, and then I heard a thump and a yelp from the back of the store. I rushed between the bookcases. The two teens stood, mouths agape, staring at a book that lay splayed spine up on the ground.

"Oh Biff," I muttered, "what now?"

I took a calming breath, and forced myself to slow down.

"What happened?"

The girls looked from me, to the book, and back to me, and then I noticed there was a small pile of books on the corner chair, and another stack on the floor, where they'd clearly been sitting.

"That book," Tabitha said. "It literally flew off the shelf and smacked onto the floor."

Tracy ran her hands up and down her arms, clutching herself as if she was cold.

"And I swear the temperature dropped right before, didn't it?"

Tabitha nodded.

"Was it a ghost?" Tracy asked. "Does the store have an actual ghost?"

Great. Just what I needed. Two excitable teens agitating Biff.

I ignored their questions and went to pick up the book. It was a different one this time; *Medieval Sorcery* was the title. Okay, so what was the connection? First the book on the household magical creatures, and now sorcerers.

"What are you trying to tell me, Biff?"

"I knew it," Tracy said. "I knew there was a ghost."

I stifled a curse. I hadn't realized I'd said those words out loud.

Well, as I'd said to Stefon, the only way out was through. I braced myself. Cradling the book in my hand, I looked at Tracy, and then at Tabitha, both of whom stood in the same posture now, arms crossed over their chests as if waiting for me to deny it.

"Yes. The bookstore has a ghost. His name is Biff and he used to own the place a long time ago."

The teens both leapt into the air and squealed like I'm sure they hadn't squealed since they were ten.

"This is so cool," Tabitha said, once they calmed down.

"Please don't tell anyone," I said.

"Why not?" Tracy said. "Ghosts are good for business, aren't they? Seems like that's what drives all the business to the Kelpie."

They were probably right. It's just that I really didn't feel like dealing with the type of tourists that came by only because of ghosts. Renting a vacation room at the Historic Kelpie Inn for a few days in hopes that you got scared in the middle of the night was one thing, but bookstores had enough trouble with lookie-loos as it was.

All the people who came in to read a few pages and then immediately ordered the book online? Those would just be joined by people who wanted to see a ghost, take a selfie in the paranormal section, and then leave.

"We could help you, you know," Tabitha said.

"Help me with what?" I really wanted to look at this book and figure out what it was trying to tell me, but I just didn't have the time.

"With ideas for bringing people into the shop—you know, around the ghost—and getting them to actually buy books. I mean"—she looked around at the empty shop—"don't you need more customers?"

"It's the slow season," I snapped. "We're always slow after the holidays."

Their faces fell, making me feel like an ogre. I relented. "But I might take you up on it, I just have to get through inventory and figure out this case first."

Both teens wisely remained quiet.

"What did you find out?" I asked.

"Well, we did research on missing faery creatures and we didn't find anything," Tracy said. "What we found was that usually it's humans that go missing, stolen by fairies, but this doesn't seem like that, does it?"

I shook my head and thumbed the book's worn

leather cover. "No, this is definitely a threat to the magical creatures, not the humans."

Except what did that say about Rolf's grandmother? As if in answer, I heard the bells at the front of the store ring, and heard Stefon's rumble and Duncan's higher response.

"Well, keep at it for a bit longer if you're not bored. I have to go meet with somebody right now."

"Okay," Tabitha said. "Tracy's mom won't be back for another forty minutes anyway. She went to get a manicure."

"All right, thanks a lot. I'll text you later for a report."

"Sarah?"

I turned back, both teens had already settled bonelessly back onto the floor, books open in their laps, but Tabitha held out a hand.

"You should give us that book," she said. "If Biff the ghost thinks it's important, we should probably look at it, right?"

I surrendered the old tome, feeling a slight tingle as it passed from my hands to hers. Definitely something there.

Thanks, Biff, I thought, then walked up towards the front, hoping against hope that things weren't about to get even more strange.

25

We were crammed into Rolf's grandmother's accessory dwelling unit. A small modern house that matched the large house Rolf lived in, it was literally in his backyard.

Why she just didn't live in the big house with Rolf, I wasn't sure. That space seemed way too large for one single man, but maybe she just wanted her own space, away from his obvious wealth and his strange, medieval re-creation friends.

She was small and thin, with pale white hair, elegantly styled. She wore a long burgundy tunic sweater over black leggings and fuzzy slippers, and she shuffled about, getting us tea that we had insisted we didn't need.

But I understood. It's the small rituals that help to keep us going when we're under stress. She looked a lot like Rolf, and had enlisted the much taller man to help carry things out from the tiny kitchen space into the cozy living room.

Once we were finally settled onto the navy loveseat and striped gold and navy armchairs, with the unwanted teacups in our hands, Rolf cleared his throat.

"Tell them, Nana."

She looked out the window at the wet, gray garden. Her pale blue eyes looked far away, as if they were seeing into someplace else, the distant past or another realm.

"I went for a walk," she said, still staring out into the garden space, "with just my jacket and my keys. I had thought I would be right back. And then all of a sudden I saw a woman who I'd never seen before, but she seemed so nice, so pretty. She asked if she could walk with me for a while. And I said yes."

She fell silent.

"And then?" Rolf prodded. "Tell them the rest, Nana."

She finally looked at her grandson, and then at Stefon, and then at me. "And then I was falling down the cliff, and then I was flying, and then I was in a cave, and then I was beneath the sea, and then..."

Her breath came in rapid pants and her already pale skin turn sheet-white. Rolf scooted closer to her on the loveseat and took her hand.

"It's okay, Nana. You're at home now, and we're all here with you."

She took in a shuddering breath, and gripped her grandson's thin hand with her own wiry fingers.

"And then I was back in the yard outside, soaking wet, without my keys. I had to go find the spare to let myself in."

Something about this wasn't adding up. I mean, not

just a strange journey she'd been taken on, or the fact that the sorcerer woman seemed to have shown up again. But the time loss, the sudden reappearance in her own yard after having been out walking.

The lack of keys.

She looked down at her pants and picked at her sweater.

Suddenly I knew she was lying. But why?

"I'm sorry Mrs. Weber, I don't mean to imply..."

"But you don't believe me," she said, still not looking up.

"Nana..." Rolf said softly. He shot me a look of reproach.

"I wonder if you're not leaving something out," I said. "Something important. Something we really need to know."

She swallowed, hard. "That woman... She was such a beautiful one with dark and silver hair. I've seen her around town and she seemed so warm and kind. She said she needed me."

"Needed you for what, Nana?"

"She said she needed a crone to complete the spell. And then I saw she had... I saw images, and I didn't know what was real. I saw two young women and an adult. One of the younger ones looked like the adult was their mother. And then I saw the small, friendly kind of spirits. Do you know the ones?" She tipped her face up to Rolf's. "The ones that keep the gardens green and healthy."

Rolf shook his head, looking at us with apology.

I held up my hand to stop him, and leaned toward

Mrs. Weber. "I know exactly the ones you mean. Please. Tell us what you saw."

"She was going to use them, somehow. She was going to use us all. She needed to right an old wrong, or something. I...my brain wasn't working quite right and I found it hard to follow it all."

"And then?" Stefon asked.

She looked up, and straightened her spine, and that same steel schooled her features. She was no longer the confused, helpless old woman who had greeted us. I saw her true power.

"I told her no."

26

Mrs. Weber pitched toward me then, and grasped my hands across the small round coffee table. Her fingers were bony, but strong. She looked at me with those eyes, blue as the softest, sky-blue silk, waving in a summer breeze.

I fell into those eyes, tumbling forward. Stefon shouted, but it was too late.

Mrs. Weber and I plunged through the sky, alternating layers of summer blue and pounding winter rain. Warm. Cold. Warm. Cold. White. Black. White. Black.

Air soft as down. Air harsh as knives.

And finally, we landed on a cliff-top promontory, set on our feet as if we hadn't just hurtled through faery or the astral planes, or wherever and whenever we had traveled. My stomach lurched, trying to catch up. My mouth tasted like metal.

Waves crashed behind us, powerful and distant. In front of us, where there should have been rocks and trees, was an eerie mist. Better than standing out in the rain without a coat, I supposed, but at the moment? I would have preferred a natural, cleansing rain over this strange environment.

Mrs. Weber clutched my arm. I guess we had dropped hands as we fell...wherever we were.

"Here she comes!" she hissed in my ear, breath puffing warm on my cheek.

And then I saw it. A dark shape, moving in the mist, forming and dissolving. Coming closer.

It resolved itself into a woman, walking.

And then the mist parted and she stepped through, aura snapping with sorcery, flaring silver, bronze, and gold. Her long, dark, silver-shot hair swirled around her fine-boned face.

It was the woman from the crystal ball. The one from Angie's café. And she was no simple Goddess worshipper.

As soon as she saw us, she lifted her hands.

I threw mine up and blasted her with all the power of the ocean at my back with one hand, and shoved Mrs. Weber aside with the other. I heard Mrs. Weber yelp as the sandy rocks to my right exploded. I leapt out of the way of a second blast, just in time.

I drew up magic from the earth beneath my feet and barreled towards the woman. She hadn't expected that, and ducked and dodged. I sent another blast, this time aiming towards her head.

With a blast of her own, our two arcs met in midair, crackling white and blue. I had never seen magic manifest like that before. What a way to claim my power again.

"Cyrus!" I shouted, hoping my voice would carry a psychic message to my uncle and he would teleport in to help. The woman grimaced and reached out and grabbed me with her physical hand. I wrestled with her, not wanting to use magic anymore, not this close up. I heard Mrs. Weber scrabbling behind me, and just hoped she stayed out of the way.

Pressure built behind my temples. Dammit. The sorcerer was trying to force her way into my head. I shoved back, hard. We both stumbled, staggering closer to the edge.

Mrs. Weber screamed and hurtled into me from the other side, forcing us away from the edge.

Thank goodness she was strong, despite looking frail.

I shoved back at the sorcerer with my mind, imagining my brain was a big talon that could reach into the sorcerer's brain to rip and rend. She shrieked.

"Who are you?" I shouted.

She grimaced and didn't reply, but inside my head I heard her whispering voice. *Thekla,* it said.

The air whirled around us, as if a helicopter was landing. And a new power joined us. One that tasted familiar. One that smelled of Bay Rum and frankincense.

Thank all the Gods and Goddesses, Cyrus had arrived.

And suddenly the sorcerer released me. She smiled, teeth bared in a feral grin, and saluted Uncle Cyrus.

And then she disappeared as quickly as she had arrived. And I was left on the promontory, lungs heaving, trying to draw in a steady breath.

Mrs. Weber was at my side. "Are you all right, honey?"

I just nodded, unable to speak. Uncle Cyrus turned to me, his face serious, his eyes scanning me, both my body and my energy fields. I felt him probing. His psychic touch was gentle, but I winced. The sorcerer had gotten a blow in, and the left side of my temple really hurt. But it was strange, it didn't hurt on the *outside* of my head; the ache was inside, as if a big hammer had struck me on the astral plane.

And that's where we were, wasn't it? The astral plane.

"You're all right," Cyrus said. It was a statement, not a question, so I didn't answer. Instead, I just lurched upright as best I could, and wiped my hands off on my jeans. My hands were damp, as if I had dipped them into the ocean. They were cold, too. I shoved them in the pockets of my jeans, which were also wet, so that didn't help much.

"Let's get you both home," Uncle Cyrus said.

He put one hand on my shoulder and the other on Mrs. Weber, and then we were falling again, falling upward instead of down, but I still could not call the sensation flying. And then quickly and much more smoothly than we had arrived, we were back in the garden between Rolf's big home and Mrs. Weber's ADU.

Stefon and Rolf barreled out of the smaller building, and Stefon grabbed me and held me close. I heard Rolf talking to Mrs. Weber and bringing her inside. Uncle Cyrus followed them. Stefon didn't move; he just held on, breathing hard, as if wrestling back some strong emotion.

It felt good to be encircled by his arms, and just to breathe for a while, surrounded by his warmth in the cold Oregon air.

27

All that inter-realm travel had exhausted Mrs. Weber, so Rolf helped her to bed.

I didn't blame her. I was tired, too. But really, I was that strange combination of tired and wired. I was also completely overwhelmed and ready to give up while simultaneously ready to head into battle again.

We were back in Rolf's amazing living room. I was curled up next to Stefon on the couch. He had his arm around me, and I was nestled into his chest and belly, a glass of Oregon Pinot Noir in my right hand.

Rolf was down the long hallway at the door, getting the pizza delivery, and Uncle Cyrus looked perfectly at home in one of the chairs next to the fire, as if he had been for a stroll in St.-Germain-des-Prés.

Rolf's wasn't a wood-burning fireplace like the one at my house, but the dancing gas flames were nice all the same. Rolf came in and tucked the pizzas on the granite kitchen countertop and started clattering about with plates and utensils. Stefon kissed my forehead and got up to help him, bringing me back a slice of chicken and arugula with pesto sauce and another slice of traditional pepperoni and cheese.

As soon as the smells hit my nose, I was ravenous. Luckily, Cyrus seemed to know I would need to replenish myself after all that magical and astral work, and waited until I had half a slice in me before clearing his throat to begin.

"Tell us what happened again, please," he said.

I chewed a piece of chicken and swallowed the tangy pizza crust. We'd been through all this once before with Mrs. Weber, but I could see that things weren't adding up. I could practically visualize the gears and cogs whirring and clicking inside Uncle Cyrus's smooth-domed head.

He hadn't shared his thoughts with us yet, which was another sign there was a lot going on with him. Cyrus held his counsel only when something was very dangerous, worrisome, or didn't quite make sense to him yet.

Or, worst-case scenario, all of the above.

I wiped my hands on a paper napkin, took another sip of wine and tried to remember. That's the thing about big magic, and astral travel, and all the rest of it: the brain can't quite make sense of it and so either it fills in the blanks with things that seemed more rational, or it just pushes whatever knowledge the brain acquired back out again.

It was sort of like that experiment where the doctor hits your knee, and you stand up and say you heard someone knocking at the door and are answering it. You never heard a knock, but your brain has filled in a plausible reason for you to be up and off the table.

As a consequence of the clashing magic and weird and sudden astral journeying, my head was filled with a jumble of emotions, sensations, and disjointed intellectual information.

"Mrs. Weber grabbed me, and suddenly we were hurtling through space. And it was a really strange combination of things. Like, when I got pulled into the cave, it was all one thing…"

"And this time?" Stefon asked, before shoving another bite of pizza into his mouth.

"This time it was as if we were flip-flopping between two very different worlds, quickly transitioning from one to the next, and back again. And then we landed where you found us. And there was a mist, like there often is on the astral plane…"

It was funny—I hadn't quite realized that at the time. My experience of the astral always began with a mist like that. I just hadn't thought of it because the Oregon Coast can be so foggy at times.

"And then?" Uncle Cyrus asked, voice sharp. I didn't blame him for being impatient with my pauses.

"And then she came out of the mist, and then all of a sudden we were fighting. And then you showed up."

"And she told you her name was Thekla."

"No." I shook my head. "Not out loud, anyway. A voice whispered it. Inside my head. Maybe it was hers, or maybe it was someone else."

I searched my memory, trying to figure it out, but got nothing.

"So, who is this person?" Rolf asked.

"An old colleague of mine." Cyrus looked as if he wanted to spit out his wine, as if the tasty Oregon red had turn to vinegar in his mouth.

"But why is she here now?" I asked, setting my plate of half-eaten pizza down on the big ottoman in front of me. My stomach was cramping with nerves, making it hard to eat.

"She's always interested in hoarding more power," he said. "But mostly, she came here to Test you."

I heard that capital T and didn't like it. Not one bit.

"That's why you came back?" My whole body flushed with anger. "You knew this was going to happen, didn't you? Some grand poobah council of warlocks and witches decided to give me a push. Is that it?"

"Sarah, I couldn't tell you. As your closest family mentor, I'm not even supposed to be here." He spread his hands in a placating gesture, his handsome face looking serious, rueful, and kind. "But yes, there is always Testing during the time of a person's first Saturn Return to make certain the witch or warlock is quali-fied to take on further duties. I knew it was your time, I just had no idea they would send *her*."

"Then why are you here?" I crossed my arms over my chest. Uncle Cyrus was not going to charm or cajole me. Not this time.

"Because I couldn't leave you fully unprotected. Yes, I didn't know they were sending Thekla as your exam-iner, but no matter who they sent, I couldn't take the risk..."

"That I would fail?"

He said nothing. Stefon cleared his throat, and Rolf

kept munching pizza, as if he was watching a particularly interesting television show.

"I don't get it," Stefon said. "If she's here to Test Sarah, why is she attacking magical beings? I mean, why not just attack Sarah directly? And besides, if she was attacking anyone, it seems like you'd be a prime candidate."

Cyrus laughed, a harsh and rueful sound.

"Oh, I am quite certain she would like nothing more than to blast me to oblivion, after stealing my power, if possible."

He stared out the large plate glass windows at the gray and glorious ocean.

"But she knows she hasn't got a chance. Also, we have no proof that it is Thekla attacking the others. If she was sent to Test you, it hardly seems likely that she would take time out to smash up greenhouses, let alone kill a dryad."

Huh. The fact that there was more than one person messing around in Seashell Cove was not comforting.

"And how about Mrs. Weber," I asked. "Was her vision all a lie?"

Uncle Cyrus shrugged. "I have never comprehended Thekla's methods. She and I have been at odds for a very long time. She may have lured Mrs. Weber out as another means to check your reflexes. Some witches are more likely to use their power to protect others, so this makes some amount of sense. Granted, this is a more elaborate Saturn Return Test than I have ever seen before, but the grand poobahs, as you call them, did think you might need something complex."

"Why?" My head swirled with this new information.

"Because of who your parents were, Sarah." Cyrus's voice was gentle now. Too gentle.

Tears pricked at my eyes, though I couldn't say whether they were tears of sorrow or anger or both.

All I knew was that, despite his explanations, none of this made any sense.

"This has something to do with my mother, doesn't it?" I asked.

He just shrugged and took another swallow of wine. I picked up my own glass and drank deeply. Stefon stared between the two of us as if he was at a tennis match. A tennis match that pissed him off.

"This isn't the right time to talk about that." Uncle Cyrus looked uncomfortable.

"When will it be?" Stefon said. "I would think that Sarah has a right to know something like that."

I patted Stefon's leg, then sat, cradling my wine glass, waiting for Cyrus to say something. Anything. Rolf looked as if he wanted to crawl out of the room, but went to the kitchen counter for another piece of pizza, instead.

"I'll tell you once you have passed your trials," Uncle Cyrus finally replied.

Well, wasn't that great? I still had a murder to solve. And I also had to pass a major Test I never even knew was coming.

Turns out? Saturn Return is a bitch. Who knew that turning twenty-eight would cause such trouble?

28

———

I needed a day off from it all, so I was visiting Cecilia at the body shop, and was perched on a short, battered stool next to an Impala in shimmering gold with sharp black detailing. The air smelled of grease and metal, and cold rose from the concrete in waves, despite the heaters that clicked and buzzed near the ceiling, and the space heater parked next to me.

Two days had gone by with not much happening. Except the fact that I'd become a nervous wreck and had a headache that wouldn't quit.

That and, despite the appearance of Thekla, I still didn't know why she was doing what she was doing. Other than "testing" me somehow.

Testing my ability to use magic on the fly? Testing my ability to go on the offensive? Testing my willingness to protect other beings, the way Uncle Cyrus had suggested?

But a dryad was dead, and there was still something after the smaller magical beings. A rogue witch, like

Toby said? I couldn't rule out Delta Crabbit, or, much as I hated to admit it, even Angie. What if she'd been messing with the garden spirits and they'd smashed it up themselves in retaliation?

Or what if—despite what Cyrus had said—it was Thekla behind it all? Rolf's grandmother seemed to think she'd seen the chaneques, but her brain had been a bit addled by being yanked around on the astral plane, so there was no telling what was real and what was delusion.

Nothing made much sense to me.

Here I finally had given myself back to my magic, was even willing to take on the mantle of Justice, and everything ground to a halt. The chaneques and Toby were still in Uncle Cyrus's safe house, but were itching to get back home.

"I miss them," Cecilia said, "but I know Seashell Cove is just too dangerous right now."

"Yeah," I replied. "They should be safer in Portland than here, but..."

Well, wasn't that foolish of me? At least I stopped myself before finishing the sentence. Cecilia looked stricken already and didn't need my "but there's danger everywhere" input.

I fell silent, and my thoughts wandered toward the teens. They were turning out to be really helpful. It's funny how it didn't take long to discount people just a dozen years younger than me, when I knew how capable my friends and I had been. Tracy and Tabitha were still digging into the books, swearing they were getting somewhere, though so far, it didn't seem that way to me. They split their time between the bookshop and helping Mr. Vargas clean up the cliff top where the dryad had been killed.

And who had killed the dryad? We didn't know that, either.

There was still way too much we didn't know.

Cecilia was bent over the engine of the beautiful classic car, a red rag stuffed in the back pocket of her faded blue coveralls. The only reason I knew the car was an Impala was the name spelled out in cursive metal letters on the trunk. She wiped her hands on the greasy rag and closed the hood with a satisfyingly heavy thunk.

"I can't work anymore," she said, "which sucks because work is usually the one thing that saves me."

I knew exactly how she felt. I had left Duncan in charge of The Widening Gyre yet again because I was just too antsy to deal with customers. Actually, it had been his idea that I leave after I almost snapped at Delta Crabbit, who had run from the shop, half in tears.

I felt like a jerk about it, but at the same time? Ms. Crabbit was still on the suspect list, even though no one but me thought she was even a player. There was just something I didn't trust about her.

Uncle Cyrus was no help. After that night at Rolf's, he up and disappeared and I hadn't heard from him since, the jerk. The only bright light had been Stefon and, surprisingly, Tabitha and Tracy.

Not only were they an invaluable help, they were keeping me distracted. And Tracy's mother, Carol, was so thrilled for them to have something to do while she was at work that she happily drove them wherever they needed to be driven. Since she worked at home, I could especially see where she wanted them out of her long blond hair.

"So you haven't felt anything since, you know?" Cecilia asked.

I shook my head no.

"It's been strange," I said. "I mean the whole thing is strange, right?"

She nodded and stepped over to the small fridge in the corner of the shop to grab a bottle of water. She wiggled it at me in question, and I shook my head no. I'd imbibed way too much liquid for the afternoon already.

"Where is everybody, anyway?" I asked. The shop was suspiciously empty.

"Oh," she said, "we're always slow after the holidays just like everyone, so I said I would take over for today so Raul could do something with his kiddos."

"That's cool," I said. Raul was her boss—we'd known him since we were teens and he was in his mid-twenties—and a totally sweet man who deserved a day off.

"I just keep feeling like the other shoe is about to drop." I nibbled on a fingernail. That was a thing I'd never done until all of this started. I'd never understood people who chewed on their fingernails and yet here I was. I took my hand out of my mouth and shoved it into my hoodie pocket.

"Isn't there anything you can do?" Cecilia leaned up against the gold car. "Like some magic or something?"

"I've tried." And that was the truth. I'd even sent Stefon home the night before so I could light some candles and try to do some magic on my own, but nothing had happened. The images on the tarot cards were silent. My pendulum remained still, no matter how long I held its chain between my fingertips. And my mother's crystal ball didn't show me a darn thing.

At least Thekla hadn't shown up with another dang part of my Test. But her absence was disconcerting, too.

Cecilia motioned me up and led me toward a couple of battered couches that were really old bench car seats grouped together in one corner of the garage. One of those big, greasy wooden cable spools served as a coffee table in the center of them. A small stack of outdated car magazines sat on top of it, along with an abandoned white coffee cup.

Cecilia flopped down onto the double seat of duct-taped burgundy. I followed suit, choosing a shiny teal blue and white bucket seat.

"So, what are you gonna do about this?" she asked, cracking open the bottle of water.

"Heck if I know. The stuff with the disappearances and the sorcerer and all the rest of it doesn't seem right."

She laughed. "Should it?"

I shook my head and looked out the open garage bay doors to the steadily falling rain.

"It's more than that. Uncle Cyrus is keeping a bunch of things from me."

"Like what?"

I stared at the rain drops falling on concrete, and at the ivy clawing its way over an old brick wall as if they held the answers. As if they could tell me what my tarot cards and pendulum would not.

I looked back at my friend who sat, jiggling a

booted foot on top of her coverall-clad knee. Her pink hair stood up in random tufts. She'd been tugging at it again, and I couldn't blame her. Not only was her lover gone, but we were no closer to solving any of this.

"He told me he'd come back to Seashell Cove because of me. Because I wasn't using my magic. But then all this terrible stuff started to happen, and now he says it's just all part of some elaborate testing period. For me. But no one would kill a dryad just to test my magical chops. Right?"

Cecilia stopped jiggling her foot. She gave me a searching look. "Do you think he knew this was going to happen? I mean, not the testing stuff, but that Toby and the others were going to be in danger?"

I stood up. I was just too antsy to sit still.

"Heck if I know. All I do know is that his excuse for leaving Paris didn't quite make sense, but I figured it was just me avoiding things as usual…. But all this stuff happening just being part of the Test, and starting right after he arrived?"

"Too big a coincidence," she said. I looked at my ex. Her eyes had that shrewd look she got when her brain was putting puzzle pieces together. That was good, because I needed all the help I could get right now.

"Way too big a coincidence," I said.

She stood and grabbed her ridiculous rainbow slicker from a hook on the wall.

"Let's go."

"Go where?"

She looked over her shoulder, already halfway to the big bay doors, and gave me one of those *What are you, dense?* looks.

"We're going to track down your uncle. This *can't* just all be about you. I'm closing the shop."

How we were supposed to track down a powerful warlock who wanted to remain hidden, I had no idea. But I wasn't about to argue with a determined mechanic with bright pink hair.

29

Before we even exited the parking lot, my phone rang. I stopped the Fiat, Cecilia's muscle car rumbling behind me.

It was Angie.

"Hey! What's up?"

Her greenhouse had been broken into again. Could I come?

I sat, staring out the windows of my little electric car, not really seeing the auto body shop. Not seeing the towering trees. Not seeing the gray sky.

Not really seeing much of anything, but trying to sense the disturbance that I knew was floating somewhere in the æthers.

Was this another part of my Saturn Return doohickie? Or was this somehow connected to the death of the dryad?

And did Angie calling mean she was off the suspect list, or was it just a way to throw me off track again?

Behind me, Cecilia honked her horn. Just a little tap, clearly asking what the holdup was.

"We'll be right there." I hung up with Angie, hopped out, and motioned for Cecilia to roll her window down. White exhaust pumped from the back of Cecilia's car. I could smell the slight burnt oil of it mixing with the fresh coastal air.

My magic senses were tingling. Witch's intuition on overdrive.

"What now?"

"We need to stop at Angie's. Her greenhouse was broken into again."

"Lead the way."

I scurried back to the orange Fiat. That was one great thing about old friends. You didn't always need to explain things.

Sometimes just saying you needed something was enough.

The auto body shop rested just south of the main drag. We rolled down the highway, cruising along the curves, with hills to the right and flashes of beach and ocean on the left.

Just ahead, on the hillside of the highway, was a large, carved wooden sign. A black horse traipsed across a large rolling ocean wave, while from below, a mighty red kraken wrapped its tentacles around letters reading *The Historic Kelpie Inn*. Farther up, on the ocean side, a row of well-anchored sidewalk pennants snapped and fluttered in incongruous shades of neon pink and yellow. *Charming Collectibles*, a sandwich board proclaimed.

As usual, Seashell Cove looked like a sleepy town,

pleasant, as charming as the collectibles would prove to be. Except the inn was definitely haunted and the collectibles might be cursed.

Turning off the highway, I found parking just off Main Street, twenty yards or so from The Blueberry Café. Angie had one greenhouse at her home, and a smaller one behind the café, next to a pocket-sized parking lot. I always forgot the lot and greenhouse were even there, because mostly I walked to Angie's place from the bookstore, getting more exercise in.

Cecilia was smarter. Her car rumbled by, heading into the lot. Locking my car, I zipped up my coat and increased my stride.

Angie had sounded pretty upset. Pissed off, actually, which was not like her.

As I rounded the corner, passing a battered green Dumpster, I heard voices.

Across the small parking lot, where only a few cars were parked, including my ex's, Cecilia stood with Angie, Carol, and both teens near the battered metal back door that led to the café's kitchen. They all wore their rain jackets, and a light breeze tugged at their clothing and hair. Speaking of which, my own hair was going to be a tangled mess soon. I pulled a burgundy beret from my jacket pocket and slipped it on. Much better.

How the teens and Carol had gotten there, I didn't know. Maybe they'd been having an afternoon snack at the café?

"What happened?" I asked, boots scattering loose gravel as I walked.

Angie, arms crossed over her purple polar fleece

jacket, blue apron flapping around her jeans, grimaced and pointed to the greenhouse.

"Oh, man."

The place had been trashed. Windows were busted, leaving sparkles of glass on the asphalt. A trail of dirt and greenery led from the door, where the lock had clearly been smashed.

"Who would want to do this to you?"

Angie shrugged. Portions of her faded blond hair escaped the blue kerchief she always wore while working. Irritated, she swept the kerchief from her head and set about retying it more firmly. "I have no idea. This town used to be safe, you know? But now I'm not so sure."

She gave a firm tug to the knot at the base of her skull.

"Any clue as to who it was?" Cecilia asked.

Angie threw up her hands. "Your guess is as good as mine. Although..."

"What is it?" My earlier agitation fled. I was suddenly preternaturally calm, as if every molecule connected to me focused on the here and now. Focused on sensing Angie, and the greenhouse, and whatever she was about to tell me.

"Well, Delta Crabbit has been in a lot lately, more than usual."

"Who?" Tabitha tilted her head in question. "Is that the kind of strange lady that comes into the bookshop?"

"Well," I replied, "you'd have to define strange. But she does come into the bookstore, yes. And she *has* seemed a little more out of it than usual."

I turned back to Angie. "Do you think she had something to do with the break-in?"

Angie tapped her finger against chapped-looking lips but didn't say anything.

I eased my way past the teens, boots crunching across the glass, to peer into the greenhouse. Sure enough, there were a bunch of uprooted plants, and it looked as if a sack of dirt had spilled.

"I don't know," Angie finally said. "I mean, I couldn't say for sure and I hate to accuse anybody, but…"

"But?" I asked, eyes sweeping the greenhouse. Looking for what, exactly? I wasn't sure, but dang it, I needed more clues.

"But if I had to suspect anyone, I'd have to say it would be her. She's been muttering a lot about trouble at the farm. Doesn't she own that Christmas tree farm outside of town?"

I nodded and stepped away from the broken greenhouse door. "Her family does, anyway. I know she's the bookkeeper for the farm."

"But what would the Christmas tree farm owner need in your greenhouse?" Tracy asked.

That was the question, wasn't it? And why would they murder a dryad? Was the tree farm in trouble? Had Delta been trying to move the nature spirit?

"Well, that's just great," I said.

"What?" Angie asked.

"Not only do we have to find my Uncle Cyrus, we also need to track down Delta Crabbit and find out what the heck is going on with her."

I looked at Angie for any trace that she was part of this. All I saw was anger and worry. Nothing that made me want to question her, though her greenhouse getting broken into twice still made zero sense.

And I couldn't help the feeling that we were running out of time. That if we didn't act quickly, not only might I get caught up in another one of these stupid "Tests," but someone else might die.

I turned to the teens and Cecilia. "I think we need to enlist Stefon and Rolf with this. And we're going to need to go to find Toby."

Cecilia huffed out a huge exhalation. "Finally. Thank the Gods."

I still had no clue what was happening, but all the threads that had felt scattered were slowly starting to weave their way towards each other. It wasn't quite a pattern. Not yet.

But regardless of whether this was part of my big Test or not, magical beings were still in danger and it looked like it was up to me and this ragtag gang of mine to figure out a way to help.

30

———

Angie herded us all inside. Luckily, it was the afternoon lull at the Blueberry Café. They closed at three o'clock on winter days anyway. Angie busied herself getting everyone cups of tea and coffee as we shoved a few wood tables together. Soon enough, Stefon and Rolf walked through the front café door. How Rolf was available at the drop of the hat, I didn't know. Must be nice to have a flexible work schedule and make enough money you could just take time off.

I sighed. I really needed to work on making The Widening Gyre more profitable. As soon as all of this was over.

A few stragglers packed up their books and laptops, thanked Angie, and headed out the door, throwing curious glances our way.

The teens practically bounced as they shucked their coats and draped them over the wooden chair backs. Tracy had texted her mother, Carol, who walked in just as Angie turned the sign to Closed. The one remaining café worker bustled quietly in the kitchen area, going through what must be the usual cleanup routine. A light rain tap tapped on the windows again, and darkness was fast approaching.

That was the one thing people who moved up from California complained about, the way winter dark came way too early and lasted entirely too long. You'd think the winter solstice would give us some respite, but it doesn't. You just had to get used to the dark and rain.

"So, I think we found something," Tabitha said.

"In that old medieval sorcery book Biff dropped," Tracy chimed in.

They yanked their chairs out, scraping them on the wooden floors. I saw Angie wince, but I was surprised she even noticed it anymore. Surely her customers weren't that careful, either.

Stefon gave me a quick kiss before he and Rolf sat down at the other end of the shoved-together tables.

"What did you find out?" Stefon asked.

"And who's Biff?" Rolf chimed in.

"I'll explain later, man." Stefon put a hand on his friend's shoulder. Rolf settled back into his chair and dumped sugar into his coffee mug.

We all looked expectantly at the two teens, who seemed super excited to have something to offer.

Tabitha leaned forward, dark eyes flashing with excitement, her black bob falling neatly around her face. "We found out that those old medieval sorcerers did call on other magical beings. To fuel their magic!"

"Sure," I said, "like demons and angels."

"No!" Tabitha bounced a little in her chair. "That's

just it. That's what we assumed it would be, but there are all sorts of stories about using imps and other small creatures. Creatures that did their bidding...."

"What did they do with them?" It was Stefon's turn to lean over the table.

"All kinds of things!" Tracy said, running fingers through her blond hair.

"Tell them," Carol said.

My hands grew cold around the warm mug and my stomach sank again.

"I think I know what they're talking about," I said.

"What's that?" Angie asked. "And what does it have to do with my greenhouse getting busted up?"

"I think whoever it is may be trying to open a portal."

"A portal to where?" Stefon asked.

He knew all about portals, at least fictional ones, from his years of role-playing games.

I was about to answer when I saw a familiar shape crossing the street. Sure enough, it was Delta Crabbit.

I shoved my chair back, spilling my tea.

"Hey!" Angie shouted.

"Sorry!"

I yanked at the lock, pulled open the front door, and ran.

"Delta!" I shouted, heedless of the fact that the rain had picked up and I was getting wet. She looked fearfully over her shoulder and started walking faster, scrabbling like a crab on the beach. I was grateful for the fact that I was a jogger and she clearly wasn't. I caught up with her in no time and nabbed the collar of her coat.

"Delta! Stop!"

"Let me go," she said, struggling against me. She carried something heavy in her canvas bag. It slammed against my legs, and I heard a squeak.

"Delta! What are you doing?" My fingers slipped on the slick protective fabric of her coat. I grabbed on more firmly.

"What are *you* doing?" Her voice was high, petulant like a child's.

Despite my hat, the rain whipped strands of wet hair against my face. My sweater was getting soaked.

"Come with me," I said.

"You have no right!" She pulled back against me, hard. We both stopped then, in the middle of the wet, empty sidewalk. My hand still gripped her coat. We were both panting a little bit.

And then I looked down and saw that her fingernails were covered in dirt.

"You stole Angie's plants."

"I didn't."

"Delta. What's in the bag?"

"I...I can't tell you that." She set her mouth in a straight line, lips pressed together.

"I really think you'd better come back with me and explain yourself to Angie."

She slumped then, as if in defeat, and let me lead her back to the café.

Angie let us in, worry marring her face.

The heat of the café and the warm cinnamon and chocolate scents surrounded me once again.

"What's happening?" Angie asked. "Why did you run off?"

"I think Delta needs to explain that to us, don't you, Delta?"

Delta just sniffed and stumbled her way through the café to the shoved-together tables.

Stefon leapt up and got another chair, motioning for her to sit as Angie went behind the counter to fill another cup of tea.

Delta took off her coat, one arm at a time, trading off gripping the canvas bag in the other hand. Finally, she sat, the bag secure upon her lap. The thing was still moving and squeaking.

Angie set a mug down in front of Delta. "What in the world is in your bag? And why are your hands all dirty—did you...?"

"Yes, *did* you, Delta?" I asked.

"You always called me Ms. Crabbit before," she said with another sniff, one hand like a claw around her mug, the other still gripping the bag. "I don't know why you're changing now. It's just rude. And grabbing me like that."

I glared. "Maybe because I was being polite before, and I don't much feel like being polite right now."

"Ms. Crabbit," Stefon said gently, shooting me a quelling look, "I think you need to explain to us what's in your bag and whether you had anything to do with Angie's greenhouse getting smashed."

She sighed, a gusty gurgling sound, as if something was wrong with her lungs. It made me wonder if she used to be a smoker. Tetris would know; he'd known Ms. Crabbit longer than any of us, and was a former smoker himself.

I forced my attention back into the café and onto

the shivering, terrified-looking woman in front of me. The wind left my sails then.

I wasn't angry anymore. I was once again just confused and upset. I couldn't get the image of the devastated hillside out of my head. Why would anyone murder a dryad?

"Ms. Crabbit, please," I said. "The chaneques are in danger and so is Cecilia's partner. And a dryad is dead."

She gasped. "It died?"

31

———

"What do you know about that?" Stefon asked, voice still soft, as if he didn't want to startle her.

"I knew something was wrong. I was trying to save it."

She turned her watery eyes to Angie.

"That's why I broke into your greenhouse the first time. I was hoping to find something to help."

"Delta?" I was incredulous. "Are you telling us you're a witch?"

She sniffed a third time. "Of course I am, you daft fool. What did you think I was?"

I just shook my head and took a sip of mint tea. All these years... I'd grown up in Seashell Cove and just thought Delta Crabbit was a regular old human eccentric. But all this time...

"Does Uncle Cyrus know? Did my dad?"

She waved her hand at me as if to dismiss my words and took a drink from her own mug.

"Your father knew. Your mother, too." She looked down into her mug, as if scrying into the liquid. "Tried to save her, too, but my magic doesn't always work right. And that fancy uncle of yours? Ha! He's not worth a bag of salt. Dismissed me, he did. Told me I was no good and I should go away."

I reached out and touched her hand. She jerked away, fragrant tea sloshing over the side. Delta shook off the wet hand and Angie quietly handed her napkin. Delta wiped off tea and mud and dirt, leaving brown stripes on the white paper.

"No one ever looks at me," she said. "No one ever thinks I can help. But that doesn't mean I don't try."

She looked at me again, piercing me with those pale brown eyes. "Every witch takes a vow, you know. You're going to have to take one soon, as soon as you're through your ordeal."

Angie put both her hands on the table and leaned forward. "Ms. Crabbit. Please. What about my greenhouse? And *what* is in your bag?"

Delta fumbled around with the canvas on her lap and slowly pulled the bag open. Up popped a peachy pale, round, little bearded face and a little purple cap covering a fringe of white hair.

Angie sat back, huffing out a breath of disbelief. "I have gnomes. In my greenhouse."

Across the table, Rolf let out a soft, "Dude."

I shot him a look, and he mimed buttoning his lips.

"I was hoping the gnomes could help the dryad, that's why I had to steal this one, because I tried convincing them before, and it wasn't working. He told me it was too late and would do no good, but I didn't believe him."

The gnome scrambled up onto the table, an angry sneer across what should have been a darn cute little face. Strike that prejudice from my roster. Gnomes could be pissed off, just like anyone else. And just because something is small, doesn't mean it's cute.

He turned, hands on his stout little hips, and stared Delta Crabbit down. "I told you it would do no good, didn't I? The dryad is already gone. Do you think we can't feel it?"

Delta hung her head and started crying softly.

"Oh, bother," the gnome said. He swiveled back to Angie. "Do you have any cookies? I'm partial to your oatmeal chocolate chip."

"You're the one..."

"Got to get my payment somehow, don't I? For keeping your herbs and whatnot growing so well?"

Angie stared at the gnome, sighed, then got up again, this time bringing back a plate of cookies for all of us to share. Everyone wisely kept their fingers away from the plate until the gnome had taken the two that he wanted, setting them on the napkin Tabitha had thoughtfully placed near his feet. He plopped down to sit cross-legged on the tabletop, and broke off a large piece of cookie.

"So, if you were trying to save the dryad," I said, "were you also the one stalking Toby and the chaneques?"

"Of course, I was. But they disappeared on me, didn't they? Before I could even ask them nicely."

"Wait? You're the rogue witch?" Tabitha said, grabbing a cookie off the big plate. "I think this seems really bad."

I had to agree, but what was next? I grabbed a cookie myself. Maybe the sugar would help me think.

"I'm not a rogue anything," Delta groused. "Just trying to do my job. Since other folks around here refuse to."

She glared at me. I returned her stare. How had I become the one to blame in this situation?

"So, what do we do now?" Rolf voiced the question.

Cookie. That's what I needed. I chewed. Chocolatey-oatey bliss. Swallowed.

"We need to do what we started out to do. Find my Uncle Cyrus."

"First things first," Cecilia said. "We're getting Toby and the chaneques. I don't care if Cyrus says his home is safe. I don't trust that the sorcerer, warlock—or whatever she is—who was sent to Test you doesn't have an agenda of her own."

"She has an agenda, all right," Delta Crabbit muttered darkly. "Those like her always do."

"All right, we're going." I turned to the teens and Carol. "I don't know about all of us trooping out there. We may need some people here, keeping the home fires lit, as it were."

"No way. You are not leaving us behind!" Tracy blurted. "Not after all we've done to help. As a matter of fact, I think we should bring Biff!"

I sighed. "That's not how it works. Biff can't leave The Widening Gyre."

"Who is Biff?" Rolf asked again.

"Not now, Rolf!" at least three people shouted. Things were getting a little tense.

"Tracy," Carol said, touching her daughter's arm. "Sarah is right. I don't want you in danger."

"That's just dumb," Tracy groused. "We could be in danger anywhere."

That was an eerie echo of the thought I'd had at the auto body shop, talking with Cecilia.

"Tell you what," I said, "if we need backup, Stefon can text you."

"But what if you're in too much trouble, and he doesn't have time to text?" Tabitha asked.

Damn, these teens were too smart. They thought of everything.

"I'm staying behind," Angie said. "You can help me look for more clues in the greenhouse, and I can use some help boarding up the broken panes."

Neither Tabitha nor Tracy seemed convinced this was a fair option. Cleaning up a greenhouse or riding off to find a bunch of magical beings? I couldn't blame them for feeling conned.

Stefon cleared his throat. "Tell you what, if you don't hear from me two hours after we leave Seashell Cove, follow us."

Tabitha and Tracy both looked at Carol, who held Stefon's gaze. Finally, Carol nodded. "That seems fair. Give me the address, so I know which way to head."

"I'm coming with you," Delta Crabbit said.

"I am too," said the gnome, though the words were muffled by the blob of cookie in his mouth.

So, there it was. We were going off to save some beings from who knew what fate.

So, rescue mission, check. But after that? How we were going to find Thekla, I had no clue. And we still needed to prove she was the one who killed the dryad, if she had. Had my testing taken a bad turn? Or had she always had an agenda, the way Delta said she did?

All I knew was that my other two suspects had just been crossed off the list.

Hopefully, Uncle Cyrus was at home. He would be, right?

Otherwise, I was on my own with a bunch of humans, a gnome, and a half-baked witch.

32

────────

I was in the back of a big luxury SUV, hurtling through dark and rain, and I didn't like it one bit. Yes, Cecilia was right, we needed to rescue the hob and the chaneques, and I wholeheartedly agreed.

But I was pissed off at Uncle Cyrus and this Thekla person. At this point, I had to assume she was the one who killed the dryad, though I could not imagine why. The last thing I wanted to do was make the almost two-hour drive inland. My hands itched to do something.

But here I was, piled into Rolf's grandmother's old Range Rover, heading inland anyway. Stefon was up front, and I was sandwiched between Delta Crabbit, who kept muttering, and Cecilia, who had been all too quiet.

From the cargo area of the SUV, the gnome quietly hummed an annoying little tune just behind my head.

The thing at the forefront of my mind—which made me more twitchy than Delta Crabbit's muttering and the gnome's humming—was not knowing if we were heading into a trap.

At least we were almost at Uncle Cyrus's home, which the map put on the west side of Portland's Willamette river. I considered this neighborhood to be Portland, but really he was just west and south of the city proper, in a cluster of fancy homes above a small lake.

Rolf piloted the Range Rover through the dark, hilly streets. The neighborhood was practically woods, the trees were so dense and varied. I could just see the diffuse twinkling of lights shining on the lake down below. Several of the large houses were also lit up, glowing from their stations set far back from the streets, often down winding driveways.

People who lived here valued their privacy, and I could see why Uncle Cyrus had made a home here, and why he thought it would be a safe place for the chaneques and the hob.

I glanced down at the map app on my phone.

"It's just right up here." I tapped Rolf on the shoulder and gestured towards the driveway opening with two lights on either side, glowing amber in the rain and gloom. I didn't see any lights farther down, which worried me. Maybe Cyrus wasn't here after all. But he had told me this was where the chaneques and Toby were hiding out...

Rolf pulled the car over and we all stared down the dark ribbon of a driveway.

Stefon turned from the passenger seat and looked over his shoulder at me.

"You sure, babe? It looks awfully dark."

It sure didn't feel as though Cyrus was here, but what else were we going to do at this point?

"This is where the address on the app is, and where Uncle Cyrus said his place was."

"We're here," Cecilia said, "and I'm not leaving until we figure out if Toby's in that house or not."

Rolf sighed, but put the Range Rover in gear and began bumping down the driveway. As we rounded a curve, there was the house, as dark as I feared. Minimalist, cantilevered decks wrapped around a mid-century modern home.

"Well damn," Cecilia said. "It really doesn't look like anyone is here."

But it didn't feel deserted.

As soon as Rolf brought the vehicle to a stop, I unbuckled and said excuse me to Delta, who quickly opened the door and hopped out. Scooching across the seat, I shoved myself out, and walked towards the house.

I stopped up short, skin tingling and buzzing, as if I'd been met by a horde of angry bees.

Uncle Cyrus's wards. I'd forgotten. I turned just as Cecilia slammed into the magical barrier and yelped.

"Sorry, I forgot to warn you guys. He has wards set up."

She touched her forehead gingerly. Ralph and Stefon walked up behind.

"Will it let us in?" Cecilia asked.

"It'll let me in for sure, because Cyrus had to know I'd be showing up here someday, if only for a visit.

What I'm hoping is that it will let you all in, but alert Uncle Cyrus something's wrong."

"You mean it's not going to scramble our insides like a transporter?" Stefon asked.

"It shouldn't."

"Shouldn't isn't good enough for me," Rolf said, crossing his arms over his skinny chest. "I'm staying here."

"Me, too," said Delta Crabbit.

"Me, three," replied the gnome.

I throttled down my irritation. Why in the world had they all wanted to come along if they weren't willing to help?

"Fine," I spat out. "I can go in on my own."

"Oh no, you're not." Stefon and Cecilia spoke at the same time.

Stefon turned to his friend. "You stay with the car. That'll be better anyway, in case we need to get away. Why don't you turn it around?"

Rolf nodded and loped back to the vehicle, clearly happy to get away from whatever weirdness was about to go down. Ms. Crabbit and the gnome took shelter beneath a bare-branched Japanese maple tree, next to the feeble glow of a solar path light. Those things weren't much good in semi-constant states of rain.

Cecilia took a deep breath and stepped forward again, bracing herself as we walked through the wards. Soon enough, we were slipping down the garden pathway toward the big dark house.

"Is that a light?" Stefon asked, keeping his voice soft and low.

I looked to where he pointed. Toward the back, around the side of the house, sure enough, something glowed.

"Let's go." I led the way, pushing open a garden gate that probably should've been locked but wasn't. That was strange. Our feet crunched on the gravel that led around to the back patio and a pool that was covered in deference to the season.

"Is there a basement?" Cecilia asked.

"It doesn't look like a basement exactly," I said. But there was clearly a ground floor back here that was tucked up against the hill, acting as a basement.

The light came from deep inside that ground floor, through glass doors that led out to gardens and a patio space.

I walk to the big, black-framed, accordion glass doors that were clearly not original to the home and peered into a big rec room, with a stone fireplace, wide screen television, and comfortable L-shaped sofa and chairs. How long had Cyrus had this place, really? And why was it decked out for entertaining?

Was he planning to move here full time?

My own reflection stared back at me through the glass.

"Does it feel weird to you?" Stefon muttered.

It did feel weird, but I didn't bother to answer. I tried the door. It was locked, so I banged on the glass

"What are you doing?" Cecilia hissed

"Finding out if anyone's home."

A ghostly face appeared deep inside the room, and Cecilia squealed behind me.

"Toby!" she said, and before I could shush her for

being so loud, Toby ran towards us, scrabbled with the lock, and flung open the door. Cecilia fell into their arms.

"You came," Toby said, head bent up to hers.

"Of course, I did," she said, mumbling into their shirt.

I cleared my throat. "Can we come inside now?"

"Oh, right. Sorry," Toby said. Separating from Cecilia, the hob backed up, making room for us to enter. And that's when I saw them, on the large L-shaped sofa. The chaneques huddled under blankets. Even in the dim light, they looked sick, as if their natural vitality had been sucked out.

"What's wrong with them?" I asked.

The one I thought of as their leader stirred and shoved himself up into a seated position, blinking at us.

Toby answered. "Cyrus said we could only go out into the garden for an hour or so a day, for safety's sake, and it's not enough. It's making them sick to be inside a building so much."

"And how long did he say you had to stay here?" Stefon asked.

Toby just shook their head. "He didn't. And frankly, we're all tired of waiting around. It's really hard to not be able to do anything. The chaneques were better off in that cave than they are here. At least they had a stronger connection to the land that they're used to."

"Oh..." Cecilia said, a hand covering her mouth. "They're dying, aren't they?"

That did it. I came to a decision.

"I don't know what Cyrus's plans are, and frankly I don't care anymore. We're getting you all out of here."

I looked at the leader of the chaneques. "We're taking you home."

Delta Crabbit wouldn't be stalking them anymore, and if Thekla wanted them? Well, she'd have to come through me.

33

This time Delta Crabbit and the gnome rode shotgun.

Toby was looking kind of queasy, but being the smallest of the adult-sized-human-types, had offered to tuck themself in the back with the chaneques. The chaneques seemed happy to cluster in the very back of the Range Rover, and were already passed out on some pillows we had liberated from Uncle Cyrus's sofa. Cecilia had the seat behind Rolf, with Toby's head tucked on the seat back, one hand on Cecilia's shoulder. I was squeezed into the center again, but next to Stefon this time. Frankly, it felt good.

While I still boiled with anger at Cyrus and what he'd done to the chaneques and Toby, sitting next to Stefon steadied and calmed me in a way I hadn't realized I needed. Badly.

One of his big hands rested on my knee, and I leaned into his shoulder as we rounded the curves through the forest. We were almost back to Seashell

Cove, having passed the big casino run by the local tribal nation about fifteen minutes back.

The Range Rover jerked, sending us skating and bumping before shooting the car into a sickening spiral.

Stefon grabbed onto me from one side and Cecilia grabbed the other. Toby braced their hands on the seat back as the chaneques yelped behind us.

The car slid down an embankment, and finally came to a stop inches from a towering spruce. The rain ticked and hissed on the hood above the warm engine block.

"What the hell just happened?" Cecilia asked.

"I have no idea," Rolf replied, panting a little. "I thought I saw something and then all of a sudden it was as if I hit a patch of black ice."

"Magic," I said out loud. "There's no black ice right now. It hasn't been cold enough. Let me out."

"Babe..."

I shoved at Stefon's mountainous bulk.

"Let me out. Now."

He complied with a grunt, shouldering open the door and stepping out. The fresh cold taste of rain hit me, followed quickly by the metallic taste I experienced only on the astral planes.

My head whipped around, looking for the warlock. The area was dimly lit by one yellow-tinged safety light up on the road.

I stepped away from the car and peered through the darkness into the trees. There was nothing but rain on needles and leaves, and the occasional whoosh of cars going by on the narrow highway.

"I know you're here," I said to the night. "But I don't know what you want."

To my left, I heard a chuckle that raised the hairs on my arms. I turned and there she was, dark hair streaming, emerging from the woods, shadowed in mist and the roiling fog where the astral plane met earth.

The air cracked behind me, as if lightning had struck. But there was no rumble of thunder. I didn't take my eyes off the woman in front of me.

She didn't look like a pleasant women's empowerment leader anymore. She looked sharp. Deadly. And her magic tasted of trees.

And then I knew.

"You killed the dryad."

"I did. There are hundreds of them here, which is why I jumped at the chance to be your challenger and Primary Tester. I've gotten three so far—they're stronger than I thought they would be. I only need two more."

"And the crone? And the teenagers?"

She shrugged. "They would have been a nice addition, but not strictly necessary for my plans. Besides, a witch like yourself? Your sacrifice will offer so much more. Too bad you won't make it through your Testing. Every so often it happens. Someone fails..."

"Thekla." A voice snapped from over my shoulder and then she laughed again. I smelled the unmistakable scent of Bay Rum and frankincense and felt Uncle Cyrus's warm, familiar magic.

"Cyrus." Thekla practically purred. "Still as handsome as always, I see. Though I think your power is slipping."

"And your power is so weak that you need to steal magic now?" His voice was measured. Careful. Low. I could barely make out his words in the rising wind and patter of rain through the fir needles.

"This is my battle," I said to him without turning.

"You're wrong," he replied. "Thekla and I have known each other a long time."

"Uncle Cyrus..."

He stepped up to stand next to me in a pile of sodden leaves, fir needles, and fallen cones, and squeezed my arm.

"This is *our* battle, Sarah. Ours."

34

———————

I heard the back of the Range Rover squeak, then slam, and the multiple thumps of what could only be the chaneques and Toby stumbling to the ground. Hopefully they were all right. Voices murmured behind me but I couldn't pay them any mind. There was too much going on in front of me.

With the sorcerer.

"What do you want, Thekla?" Uncle Cyrus's voice cracked through the rainy air.

"What I've always wanted, Cyrus. More power. And you."

"What?" The word crashed past my lips. She'd always wanted *him*? That was a really weird response. Like, did she *want* him, want him? Or want his power? Or...? My uncle had a lot of explaining to do.

"I thought once she was out of the way, you would come to your senses," the sorcerer said.

I had no idea who this *she* was. It didn't sound like she was talking about me. All I knew was that Uncle

Cyrus stood immobile at my side. It was as if he were a statue, frozen in place.

I chanced a glance over my shoulder, and Stefon shot me a subtle thumbs-up gesture. That was good: they were up to something back there. Hopefully something that would actually help.

I sank my energy deep into the soil beneath me and reached up for the rain in the trees. The powers of nature were once again accessible to me.

I choked back a sob, not realizing until that moment how much I had missed this. This feeling of being one with the world around me. Sorrow had stolen my magic and all of this connection had sunk into oblivion along with it.

Stefon stepped forward now. I felt him. Felt his strength. He was just a man, not a sorcerer, a magician, or a witch. But he was a warrior, and he was my lover and my friend. That counted for a lot right now.

I felt the earth beneath my feet shift and had no idea what was happening at first. Then I realized it must be the chaneques drawing strength from the soil and the plants. I hoped they were able to recover enough in time to help me. Because I didn't trust that Uncle Cyrus would. He still hadn't moved.

"My uncle is his own person," I said, trying to stall for time. Hoping against hope that Toby, Cecilia, and the chaneques would figure out something, and get into position. We needed an energetic shift, and I wasn't sure what would break Cyrus out of his stupor.

"You took her." Cyrus's voice was a harsh croaking sound that I hated the instant I heard it. It was the hideous scraping of a fork across the plate. The skittering of claws on marble. "She was my student, and my best friend. And you *took* her."

The sorcerer's eyes were fixed on me.

"Your Uncle Cyrus doesn't know what's good for him, and he never has. And your mother…"

A flash of anger shot up my spine and down my arms, filling my fingertips with a magic that flashed and cracked, ready to cast a lightning bolt as if I were a warlock myself. But I wasn't a warlock; I was a witch. And I wasn't sure which of my powers I needed just yet.

"What about my mother?"

"She was as stupid and ineffective as you are. Oh, beauty runs in your family, I'll give you both that. You're bright and attractive to those who should know better. But weak. Filled with uncertainty. Relying only on *love*."

She said that final word as if it were a filthy, disgusting thing, or as if she were voicing a curse. A curse that had leveled itself at her. There was something there….

Stefon drew closer and placed a hand on my shoulder. He gave me a slight squeeze and murmured, "We got you, babe. Do what you need to do."

And then I felt it. All the love he was pouring into me. All the love I had avoided receiving fully until now.

I opened every pore of my skin, every subtle energy field, every blood vessel inside my body. I opened all the way up to Stefon. To his love. And I felt that mingle with the power of earth and sky inside of me. I felt it with all of my magic. My whole being.

The ground beneath me shifted once again, the chaneques doing their magic.

I breathed the scent of tea brewing and toast toasting. And then the machine oil and sunshine that signaled Cecilia and Toby, joining the fight.

"Cyrus!" I shouted. I shot bolts of love his way. I heard him gasp, then felt him shudder. Then his magic returned with a rush and suddenly, he loosed a fireball from his right hand. Aimed directly at the sorcerer, it shot through the rain.

She shrieked and cackled and shot a bolt back at Cyrus.

He returned volley, and back and forth they went, again and again. I was transfixed by the beautiful power of their display. Two equals, matched.

The way my parents must have been.

Stefon squeezed my shoulder again.

"Babe," he said, voice taut and urgent.

It was time.

35

It was definitely time, but for what? The moment needed action, but how?

I didn't want to get between Cyrus and the sorcerer, and I wasn't sure what the chaneques were up to, or that gnome.

I scanned the dark woods and felt the power of the falling rain. I allowed myself a few seconds to just breathe in, and feel Stefon's strength at my back, and the love of everyone gathered here.

Well, except for the sorcerer.

I saw a space open. A spot between two big trees in the darkness, it was just past the stream of magic flowing between the sorcerer and Uncle Cyrus. If someone could get through that gate, it seemed like...

Before I could finish my thought, the squeal of tires came from the road, and then slamming doors and running feet.

"What the heck?" Stefon muttered, and turned. I

turned too, breaking my attention away from the magical battle.

The two teens and Carol, Tracy's mother, ran and slipped down the hill through the mud and bushes and branches. They all wore their dark Pacific Northwest coats and the teens' faces glowed with excitement, lit by the fire bolts and sparks flying through the air.

"Cool!" Tabitha said. Did teens still say that? I guess they did.

"You didn't text us, and no one was answering their phones, so we came!" Tracy shouted. "We found you!"

Carol raced forward, barely out of breath. She must be a jogger, too.

"How can I help?"

"Help?" I asked. I felt suddenly as if everyone else had a script except me.

"That warlock woman murdered the dryad," said Tracy.

"And we think we know why," Tabitha chimed in. "It's like we said, at the café…"

"There's no time for that right now, girls," Carol said. "We have a crisis in front of us. It's too late for talking."

"I wanna know everything," I said, "but she's right. Not now."

I turned to Carol. A blond curl sweeping over her forehead lit up every time a bolt of magic past. Her face was half shadowed by her rain hood, but what was visible was glowing. From the inside.

"What are you?" I asked.

She smirked. "Thought I was just a soccer mom, didn't you? Well, I am one, but I'm also a witch."

"How the heck?" I didn't bother finishing. I *knew* how the heck. I had missed it because I was still wallowing in self-pity and my own damage when she had walked through the bookshop doors.

"Great," Stefon said, then looked at me. "We need reinforcements. And the chaneques are recovered just enough, so we have help there, too. Plus, the hob."

"And us." Delta Crabbit stepped forward, the purple-hatted gnome riding on her shoulders.

"And a couple of humans that aren't afraid to fight," Cecilia said, walking up beside us. Toby came to stand at Cecilia's side.

I noticed Rolf, half hovering, as if he still wasn't sure about all of this. But he was here, and that counted.

Uncle Cyrus grunted. "I need some help here."

I ignored him for the moment and turned to the ragtag group surrounding me. The plan was suddenly crystal clear. Whether it would work or not remained to be seen. But some plan is better than no plan at all.

"Okay," I said, "here's what we're going to do."

36

The chaneques fanned out, forming a crescent around Uncle Cyrus. The hob and the teens ran through the rough gateway I'd found between the trees, followed by Cecilia and Stefon. Carol and I skirted around to the other side, flanked by Delta Crabbit and the gnome, hoping to sneak up behind the sorcerer. I could smell Uncle Cyrus's magic as it crackled and hissed. The Bay Rum and frankincense smelled a little charred around the edges.

I glanced at him as we swept by. His usually healthy and glowing skin looked a little faded. And it wasn't just the rain and the night.

He spared me half a glance and threw another fire bolt at the sorcerer.

"On the count of three," I said to him, "we're taking over."

I thought the words—throwing them into his mind—more than I spoke them out loud, but he gave a quick nod to show he understood.

"Are you sure this will work?" Carol asked.

"Heck no," I replied.

But it was the only thing I knew to try. I just hoped that between humans and the magical creatures—plus three witches and a warlock—we could defeat this bitch.

Uncle Cyrus and the sorcerer seemed to be at a stalemate. Maybe they were *too* evenly matched.

Or maybe she was up to something else?

I was counting on the strange chaos of our ragtag group to defeat her power. But putting your beliefs into action toward an outcome? Every magic worker knows there's no way to tell exactly what will happen. There is no way to assure any outcome; all you can do is make your best effort and hedge your bets.

More than that, magic requires a bit of scientific method. In other words: there was simply no way to tell what would work and what wouldn't without trying and there was no other time or place to experiment with my wacky idea. Sometimes you had to try things in the middle of a fight.

I opened up my senses and tried to track where the teens and the others were. I got a dim impression of Stefon, but that was it. And I could see the chaneques —they were definitely in position and looking much better than before. Good. Clearly, being in the woods was helping them regain their power.

I just had to hope it was enough.

Next to me, rain streaming down her upturned face, Carol chanted a silent prayer to the sky. The power flowing into her was palpable. She glowed now, taking on the sheen and shine I'd missed before.

I guess that was the sign I was waiting for.

"My name is Sarah Endora Braxton!" I shouted into the wind and rain. "You killed my mother. Prepare to die."

Bad joke? Maybe. But sometimes you need to whistle in the dark, you know?

Thekla didn't even glance at me. Probably hadn't even heard my words. I didn't care. It was long past time to deal with her.

"One!" I shouted, hoping my voice carried over the sound of the rain and the crackle of magic.

"Two!"

I braced myself and opened myself as fully as I could to earth and sky, and to my inheritance from both my parents, the line of witches that had come before me.

"Three!" The sound of the number hung in the air, and Carol and I both pulled, and the chaneques pulled, and Toby and Delta Crabbit and the gnome lent us their strength, and all together we shoved our magic toward the sorcerer as the teens, Stefon, and Cecilia barreled out from the woods and tackled Thekla to the muddy, spruce-and-fir-needle-strewn ground.

Thekla fired off another blast as she hit the ground. It barreled straight towards me. I yelped and leapt into the air as Carol dove to the side. I smelled melting rubber as the magic passed beneath my feet.

Arms windmilling, I lost my balance as I hit the muddy forest floor again. Fell. Smacked the ground, hitting my shoulder hard and jarring my head.

I grayed out briefly and came to with the rain in my face and Stefon leaning over me. Laughter burbled from my lips, though I wasn't sure why. I inhaled rainwater, and my laughter was replaced by a choking cough.

"You okay, babe?"

I looked up at Stefon's face, amazed that I could even see him in the darkness now that the magic had receded. But he was shining, too. Maybe he always shone that way, and I just hadn't noticed before.

"I will be," I said. "Thekla?"

"Delta, Cecilia, and the teens are on it. Rolf had some tie downs in his SUV that should do to keep her arms and hands bound. Meanwhile," he grinned, "the chaneques have Thekla pinned to the ground. Carol is tending to Cyrus. Everyone's okay."

"Good," I croaked. "And Stefon?"

He looked down at me. Yep. Definitely shining. Or maybe it was just the light from way up on the road.

And maybe I had a concussion, and my vision was wonky.

"Yeah, babe?"

"I love you."

It was his turn to laugh now, a surprised, warm chuckle that I felt all the way down to my toes.

"I love you too, babe. But I really want to go home. And really? You killed my mother, prepare to die?"

I would've shrugged, but it hurt too much.

37

But before we could get home, there was something else that needed doing, and I knew it.

I knew it as if it was my Goddess-ordained destiny, and dang it if part of me still didn't want to shove it away.

"Help me up."

Stefon did, gently, half lifting me until I was standing. I wouldn't be sturdy on my feet for quite some time, but standing would have to do for now.

"Where's Cyrus?"

"Over there." Stefon pointed to where Carol was crouched. Her jacket hood had fallen off and her blond hair caught the feeble light filtering down from the road.

I looked behind me, to where Thekla lay, immobile in a divot of fir needles, leaves, and mud, well wrapped in Rolf's tie down straps.

"Someone make sure she's still breathing," I said.

Rolf and Toby scurried forward. I left it to them.

"She's not dead?" someone asked, though I didn't know who. All my concentration was on the task at hand. The work that Uncle Cyrus and I still had to do.

Thekla was far from dead but that was just as well. Alive, she would face the justice she deserved. Even at a distance, I felt her pulse as surely as my own. Huh. That must be another latent talent shaken loose. At any rate...

"Help me," I said to Stefon. "I have to get to Cyrus. We have work to do."

"Babe, he's in no condition...."

I waved a hand at him and he immediately shut up. Smart man.

Tucking an arm around me, he slowly moved toward Cyrus and Carol. I leaned into him, wincing with every creak of my legs, torso, and arms. I had messed myself up good and wasn't even one-hundred percent sure how.

What can I say? It had been a long few days.

"Cyrus."

My uncle blinked up at me, then struggled to rise.

"She still alive, then?"

I nodded. We both knew exactly what we were talking about.

He pushed up and, with Carol's assistance, got to his feet.

"Let's do this," he said.

Old Sarah would have said we were a pitiful-looking crew of injured, worn out witches, and one warlock, staggering back toward Thekla—followed by the nature spirits, a hob, a gnome, and a couple of teens.

But new me?

This Sarah Endora Braxton would say we were not pitiful at all. We were strong. We had survived.

And we were there to reckon justice for a dryad—maybe three—who had never done harm to any creature, large or small. And for my mother, dead from some co smbination of jealousy and greed, it seemed. I would get the full story from Uncle Cyrus later, if it took a whole bottle of fancy wine.

The short journey was agonizing, what with my creaking bones and pounding head, but finally, we stood over the fallen witch, who scowled and spat from the mud. It looked like her headache was at least as bad as mine, though, so that gave me some satisfaction.

Cyrus was silent. I had a feeling he was waiting on me. And sure enough, a pressure built inside my bones, pushing on my heart and lungs, willing me to speak.

To speak the words that every magic being who seeks to right a wrong must speak.

Out loud.

Huh. This must be the power of being a Justice. Because I had no idea what I was going to say, but the words tumbled forth anyway, filled with the force of magic.

"Thekla. You have killed with magic, in the name of magic. Because of this, you must pay the price."

"So, kill me, then." How I had ever mistaken her for a kindly, benign, harmless Goddess worshipper, I did not know. Right now, all I saw was a face twisted by many years of hate.

Cyrus held out his right hand, palm out.

"No. That, we shall not do."

His gesture shut her up. I wasn't sure if he'd magicked her silent, or she just had no more to say.

I inhaled the damp night air. Settled my boots more firmly beneath me. Called upon the power of day and night, earth and sky, water and fire. Seen and unseen.

I expanded my consciousness, and allowed the power of Justice to speak through me once again.

"Thekla, we bind you from causing further harm, with magic, mind, or body." I raised my voice to carry. "We speak these words of magic, so every being in every world shall know: your magic shall be stripped from your bones, and you shall be required to make amends to the dryad clan. You have also killed a witch, and must face reckoning for that, as well."

"What is the payment, so that it may be recorded?" Uncle Cyrus spoke into the night. His voice was resonant. Strong.

"Thekla, formerly a sorcerer and warlock, must plant three thousand trees. And one of them must be a mighty oak, planted in my mother's name. And you must nurture these trees until the day you die."

"And it is done," Cyrus replied.

"And it is done!" As I echoed his words, I realized that every being in that stretch of woods off the side of the road spoke them with me.

And I was now my parent's child, in word and deed.

Like it or not, I had taken up the mantle of Justice. Now I just had to figure out what that meant, and how to wear the darn thing.

38

———

The tamale parlor felt full. It was closed to the public, but every one of us who'd been involved in taking down Thekla was there. We all took turns helping ferry food out of the kitchen, and there were glasses of hibiscus tea, horchata, and margaritas for those who could handle their tequila.

I'd helped with the first rounds of drinks and then Mrs. Vargas insisted I sit. I *did* seem to have a mild concussion or something that messed with my head, so I didn't protest too much.

Rolf and the teens seemed happy to take on the bulk of the serving, anyway. The rest of us clustered around the tables that had been shoved together, making one long serape-and-glass-covered table for an ad hoc family gathering. The chaneques and the gnome sat on booster seats, happily munching on peppers and spicy pickled vegetables.

Stefon's arm rested along the back of my chair, and he was in the process of feeding me a chip loaded with tomatillo salsa. A margarita glass sweated in front of me, though really it was Stefon's. Having a concussion meant I really shouldn't drink. Uncle Cyrus sat, cool as anything, across the table. He was looking much better, thank the Gods and Goddesses.

"Did you ever figure out what Thekla really wanted?" I asked once I finished chewing.

He shook his head. "I need to do some digging in the archives to figure it out, and look into what the teens found. They still think she wanted the smaller magical beings to boost her magic, and the dryad would also give her a certain power over the land. But while there is certainly power in the sort of magical beings she targeted, it isn't the usual power a sorcerer wants. They tend to go for the big, flashy payoffs."

A few seats down, the chaneque "leader" or whatever he was, signed something. Cyrus looked surprised.

"You know, I think you just may be right about that. Is there a reference I should check, or some other way to get confirmation?"

The chaneque signed again, and then nudged one of his friends, whose fingers moved, rapid-fire, in the air.

"What are they saying?" I finally asked, taking a sip of margarita, before Stefon raised an eyebrow, and replaced it with a glass of milky horchata.

"They seem to think that it has something to do with the dryad's ability to flourish under harsh conditions. The rockiest, sandiest, soil. Brutal winds."

Understanding bloomed inside me. "Dryads—and the chaneques, too—have the ability to tap into growth where the rest of us would give up. That's some pretty deep magic. Not flashy, but powerful."

"Huh," Stefon said. "Do you think her own magic was fading?"

"That's exactly what I think. She must have tapped your mother, all those years ago...." Uncle Cyrus's eyes filled with pain. "And that's what I was going to tell you, Sarah. I didn't know who it was, but something about your mother's death didn't sit right with me, in the end. So, I started investigating. Quietly. On my own. I became convinced it was some sort of baneful magic."

"Why didn't you tell me?"

"You were dealing with too much already. With your father. Besides, I didn't want to say anything until I was sure. Until I could prove something. I'm so sorry."

I set down the icy cold drink back down and clutched Stefon's hand, trying to get warm. A cold rage filled me. "Sorry for what? You didn't kill Mom."

"No," Cyrus replied. "But I didn't save her, either. Because I didn't notice what was happening until it was already too late. And I thought Thekla was just jealous of your mother's talent. None of us even noticed your mother was slowly being drained. We thought it was an ordinary, human sickness."

We both took a drink, pondering, then Cyrus spoke again.

"I think it started out that way. As a human ailment. I think Thekla saw her chance. She used the sickness as a cover and started siphoning your mother's power. That must be why, no matter how many healing spells your father and I did..." He paused. "We couldn't save her."

Stefon shifted in his chair, sitting straighter. "So, what are you going to do about it now?"

Cyrus's head snapped toward Stefon, as if he'd been slapped.

"I'm going to find a way to make it right. I'm going to stay closer this time and dig through the archives until I find some better answers. Perhaps I'll take the teens on as research assistants."

Down at the other end of the long table, the teens perked up and nudged each other, clearly listening in.

"I still don't think this is your fault," I said. "I think it's Thekla's fault. And heck, maybe even Mom and Dad's."

"Do not say that, mija." Mrs. Vargas was at the table, pulling out a chair. "Your mother and father were good people. Strong people. They did their best, all the time. They helped a lot of people."

"Then why didn't they see what was going on? Why didn't they know?"

Mrs. Vargas shook her head. "Just because someone has power does not mean they are all-powerful, or all-knowing. There is nothing that has that much power."

"And anyone who tries, has to fall," Stefon said.

I looked at him surprised. He just shrugged.

"I study a lot of history. Happens over and over again."

"Besides, sickness can take any one of us, at any time. Not one of us is immune to disability or death." Mrs. Vargas took a sip of her own horchata, then pushed back her chair and headed toward the kitchen once again.

Conversation resumed around us, though I did not

take part. Too many half-formed thoughts swirled through my aching head. I wasn't sure I'd understand what happened in that patch of forest for a very long time.

"Congratulations, Sarah," Uncle Cyrus murmured.

"On what? I'd say that was a group effort, wouldn't you?"

"For passing your ordeal. You are now a full-fledged witch in good standing and can join the council if you wish."

"I don't think so. But thanks." My parents had never seen fit to join the council, and frankly—other than Cyrus—they seemed like a bunch of stick in the muds to me. Besides... "I think I have enough on my plate right now."

"Fair enough," Cyrus replied.

"You'll help me, right?" I asked.

His dark eyes held mine for a moment. "Of course."

Our conversation was interrupted by the clatter of dishes and the most tantalizing smells of rich beans, savory meats, and piles of grilled vegetables. Soon, dishes filled with nourishing food were being passed down the long table. My stomach growled.

Even without all the answers—even in the midst of a lingering sense of loss—life called.

I shoved my chair back and stood, raising my glass. All motion at the table stopped for a moment, and then there was a flurry of glass filling and raising.

"To magic!"

"To magic!"

"To friendship!"

"To friendship!"

"To family, found or otherwise!"

"To family!"

I drank deeply, feeling the soothing taste of cinnamon and sweet rice milk. And wasn't that what life itself was about? Appreciating sweetness wherever and whenever we can? I raised my glass for one more toast.

"And to life!"

"To life!"

Everyone drank.

I sat back down and gave Stefon a firm smack on his big, warm lips.

Then I proceeded to eat the most delicious meal I'd ever had, enjoying every bite.

*W*ant to know what happens next?

The Seashell Cove ghosts are in an uproar, and centaurs have been seen close to town. Check in with Sarah, Stefon, Rhiannon, and the teens in Haunted Witch.

T. THORN COYLE
AUTHOR OF THE WITCHES OF PORTLAND
HAUNTED WITCH
A SEASHELL COVE
PARANORMAL MYSTERY

ACKNOWLEDGMENTS

Thank you to Chris and Bonnie for checking my cozy levels early in the process! Thanks to Leslie and Jack for reading, to Dayle for editing, and to Robert and Jonathan for years of support. Thanks to Dean and Loren for Kickstarter help.

And speaking of which, thank you to the 324 people who took a chance on my paranormal cozies for freaks and geeks. I'm speechless with gratitude for the support!

Most of you are listed below. For those anonymous ones who wanted no credit? Well, Rhiannon and Sarah know who you are.

A big, Kickstarter thank you to:
Abigail M. Fellnor, Adrian Emerson, Ahmarah, Aahzmandius, Alesia, Alexandra O'Bryan, Alison Naomi Holt, Allie Gentry, Alyson, Amara Snively,

Ambar, Amy Montarbo, Andréa María, Angela Raincatcher, Anna McCluskey, Anne E. Lynch, Annelise F.M., Annie Reed, Aramanth, Arianne, Becca, Becca K., Bonnie Elizabeth, Book Bunny, Breann Carpenter, Bookwyrmkim, Brad Snyder, Brendan "HollyKing" Leber, Brendon Reece, Bridgette Findley, Brooke Pratt, Carey Oxler, Carol, Carolyn Rowland, Carrie Boon, Cate Kneale, Catherine, Catriona, Céline Malgen, Bryn Hofmann, Celine, Charlie Boehme-Byrd, Chassidy Strege, Cheryl Hammond, C. F Linnds, Chris Kaiser, Chris Paton, Christina Terhune, Cintia De Carvalho, CJ, Claire Manning, Claudia Nymphenkuss, CM Wolf, Colby Smith, Constance, Crystal, Dagmar Baumann, DL, Daniel J. Riddle, David H Hendrickson, Dawn McMorrow, Dayle Dermatis, Deanna Stanley, Debbie Mumford, Deb Bodeau, Deft, Della Keeley, Diana Deverell, Diane M Smith, Dianne M. Daniels, Diva Style Minister, E., E. Scott, E Dimopoulos, Efoy, Emily Pedersen, Emily, Emma Shelford, Enfys Book, Eric & Carla Chamberlin, Erin, Erin Ratelle, Erin, Faerie Sarah, Felicia Fredlund, Fennec Foxfire, Gemma, Georgette Paxton, Gertjan, GhostCat, Glenda Nowakowski, Goldie, Greenraven, Gwells, Hal, Hannah Golden, Heidi Moone, Helen Bridget Adeline Eastwood, Helen Hawk, Henry Espy Roberts, H Alexander Perez, Hobbit, Holly, Honoré Artaud, Imani J Dean, Inanna Hazel, Amy Laurens, Iris, Ivo Dominguez Jr, Izzy Hanelt, JK, Jim Gotaas, Jamie Forster, Janet Ní Shúilleabháin, Janette Fletcher, Janine Cobb, jaymi elford, Jeanna, Jeannine, JS Groves, Jenett, Jennifer Beltrame, Jennifer Bramhill, Jennifer, Jennifer Forness, Jennifer Mroz, Jessica F, Jessica Johansen, Jessica Marquardt, Jess

Werner, Jinx, JoAnn, Johanna Rothman, John Bell, John Deltuvia, John W. Luther, Jon Auerbach, Jonathan Korman, Joe Cleary, Jaeelle Hayes, Julia Levine, Kajtryna, Karen Dougherty, Karen Snodgrass, Kat Humphries, Kate Pavelle, Kathryn F, Katina Clarke, Katy Manck – BooksYALove, Kaye & Sand, Kelly Chang, Ken Irwin, Kendall B, Kerry Paolucci, Kickstarter Music, Kim Z, Kirsten M. Corby, Kri O'Kellas, Kristen Gehrke, Kristin Rollins, Ladypants, Lanette Miller, LaRena Rose, L. E. Knight, Leslie Claire Walker, Lezlie Revelle Zucker, Lilith, Liluri, Lily Wolthers, Lindsay DelGrosso, Lisa Costello, Lisa Sanger Blinn, Lora Shimer, Loren L Coleman, Lorelei Sherman, LaffingKat, Louisa Swann, Louise Lieb, Leigh Saunders, Mackensey S, Maddie, Maggie Fry, Mambo Chita Tann, Mar Azul, Margaret, Margit Hofmann, Marian Phillips, Marine Lesne, Marissa Schwartz, MoonCrone, Mark Carter, Mary Jo Rabe, MaryAnne, Matt Fabian, Maya Kate, Megan Potter, Merri Anne Stowe, M.G. Herron, Meyari McFarland, Michael Warren Lucas, Michelle Bryant Barbeau, Michelle Mishmash, Minkenstein, MJ Silversmith, Monica Van Steenberg, Morpheus Ravenna, Myke Johnson, Karen Fonville, name, Nancy Sloop, Nate Hernandez-Botma, Nathania Apple, Neil Coles, Niall Gordon, Nicole Lynch, Nicolina, Odd, Oliver Peltier, OwlLight, Phoebe Miller, pjk, Polly, POTU David, Author, Purple Steam Dragon, Quinn Kelly, R. Hunter, Rachel Peterson, Raven Cornelius, Rebecca Hiatt, Renee Rice, R.S. Kellogg, Rebecca M. Senese, Roxan, Richard A. Loftus, Richard Hoffman, River Roberts, Rob Vagle, Robin Hill, Rosalynde, Rrrose, Ru Temple, Ruth Wotton, Ryan M. Williams,

Sage, Sage Cara, SallyRose Robinson, Samantha Landstrom, Sanchini Family, Sandra Choate, Sandra H, Sandra Mueller, Sanguine Kitty, Sara Blackthorne, Sara Ontiveros, Sarah, Sarah Underwood, Sarah A., Sarah Clark, Sea, Sea Queen, Shannon Davis, Sharon H, Sharon Rowse, Silke, Sioux Rowan, Skayle Bloodwomon, Sky Fowler, Simone P., Somcak, Sophia, souljacker85, Steph Wetch, Stephen VanWambeck, Stephanie Longoria, Stephen Ballentine, Steven Whitacre, Steve Locke, Sunshine, Susanne Winter, Tasha Turner, Taylor Morich, Teri Moody, Thalassa, Thea Hutcheson, Thealandrah, Tina, T.L. Merrybard, Tony Malerich, Tony Rella, Tracy Eire, Two renegade Appalachians, Tyler Spencer, Visucien Fe, Valerie Herron, Valkyrie, Victoria S., Violet Twilight, Wendy Williamson, Will Gwaltney, Yuu Gamon

ALSO BY T. THORN COYLE

Fiction Series

The Panther Chronicles (Complete)

To Raise a Clenched Fist to the Sky

To Wrest Our Bodies From the Fire

To Drown This Fury in the Sea

To Stand With Power on This Ground

The Witches of Portland (complete)

By Earth

By Flame

By Wind

By Sea

By Moon

By Sun

By Dusk

By Dark

By Witch's Mark

The Steel Clan Saga

We Seek No Kings

We Heed No Laws

We Ride at Night

Seashell Cove Paranormal Mysteries

Bookshop Witch

Haunted Witch

Tarot Witch

Non-Fiction

Evolutionary Witchcraft

Kissing the Limitless

Make Magic of Your Life

Sigil Magic for Writers, Artists & Other Creatives

Crafting a Daily Practice

ABOUT THE AUTHOR

T. Thorn Coyle has worked in strange and diverse occupations, and been arrested at least five times. Buy them a cup of tea or a good whisky and maybe they'll tell you about it.

Author of the *Seashell Cove Paranormal Mystery* series, *The Steel Clan Saga*, *The Witches of Portland*, and *The Panther Chronicles*, Thorn's multiple non-fiction books include *Sigil Magic for Writers, Artists & Other Creatives*, and *Evolutionary Witchcraft*.

Thorn's work appears in many anthologies, magazines, and collections. They have taught magical practice in nine countries, on four continents, and in twenty-five states.

An interloper to the Pacific Northwest U.S., Thorn stalks city streets, writes in cafes, loves live music, and talks to crows, squirrels, and trees.

Connect with Thorn:
www.thorncoyle.com